"Stop fighting the inevitable, Kara."

Kara's eyes flashed in reply. "Inevitable? I see nothing inevitable about having an affair with you, Aleko."

"You don't? Aleko smiled as though he had sensed Kara's lie. "You think I don't know that deep down inside you crave fulfillment?" he whispered as his arms imprisoned her. "Don't fight what is right and natural."

"Don't fight!" Kara demanded heatedly, furious that feelings she'd tried so hard to stem filled her with tingling excitement. "Men are all the same. They only want a woman's body. They don't give a damn about her emotions!"

"So you plan to shut men out of your life forever?"

"It depends whether I *ever* meet one I can trust," Kara snapped, pushing him away.

"Thanks for the vote of confidence," Aleko snarled, "though I fail to see how you reached such a decision about me."

MARGARET MAYO began writing quite by chance when the engineering company she worked for wasn't very busy, and she found herself with time on her hands. Today, with more than thirty romance novels to her credit, she admits that writing governs her life to a large extent. When she and her husband holiday—Cornwall is their favorite spot—Margaret always has a notebook and camera on hand and is constantly looking for fresh ideas. She lives in the countryside near Stafford, England.

Books by Margaret Mayo

MARGARET MAYO

a painful loving

Harlequin Books

TORONTO • NEW YORK • LONDON
AMSTERDAM • PARIS • SYDNEY • HAMBURG
STOCKHOLM • ATHENS • TOKYO • MILAN

Harlequin Presents first edition September 1988
ISBN 0-373-11108-8

Original hardcover edition published in 1987
by Mills & Boon Limited

CHAPTER ONE

How could life be so cruel? Kara watched the man as he strode through the Heathrow terminal. He had the same towering height, the same breadth of shoulder, the same dark almost black hair, straight and short, emphasising the strong shape and proud angle of his head.

He was in a hurry, as was the girl coming in the opposite direction. Neither saw the other until they collided. The girl, tall and starkly beautiful, was not pleased. She eyed the man angrily, but within seconds her mood changed.

Kara could not see the man's face, but she could guess at his smooth line of patter. The fault was his, his alone, it was inexcusable, he should have looked where he was going. Was she all right? Not hurt? To make amends perhaps she would join him for a cup of coffee? She didn't have time? At a later date, maybe?

That was precisely how she had met Greg—it was like looking at a replay of her own life. Except that this girl had red hair instead of blonde, this girl was five foot nine easily, compared to her own five four. But she had instantly fallen for Greg's seductive charm and ready tongue. The collision had been the beginning of an exciting relationship.

The couple parted now, each going their own way. The man did not give her so much as a backward glance; he had played this scene many times before. But the girl stopped and looked thoughtfully, almost hungrily after him. Don't be a fool, was Kara's silent advice. Don't ever get involved with a man like that.

The plane flew between green mountains silvered by a hot sun, over a bay busy with pleasure craft, and on to the runway at Corfu airport. The arrivals lounge was hot and airless and the wait for her luggage interminable. Kara felt tired and cross, and it was nothing like the last time she was here. Or was it because on her honeymoon she had noticed none of this?

And there was that man again—talking to yet another beautiful girl. Had he been on her flight? Why hadn't she noticed? Kara frowned and dragged her eyes away, relieved when she spotted her suitcase.

Sharon had instructed her to take a taxi to Corfu harbour and a boat to the island. There was no regular ferry service to Lakades, but always someone willing to earn a few drachmas. Getting a taxi, however, was easier said than done. Twice she was beaten at the last minute.

'*Despinis*, perhaps you'd like to share with me?'

Relief flooded through Kara, until she turned and encountered the dark eyes of the man she had already condemned. It was a shock to discover he didn't look like Greg after all. He had the same build, and his profile was strikingly similar, but face to face he was totally different.

This man had stronger features, though Greg's hadn't been weak. He had a granite jaw and a wide mobile mouth, jutting brows and an aquiline nose. He looked tough, as though he could be ruthless as well as charming, a dangerous enemy—as well as an exciting lover.

Her smile faded. A tremor of sexual awareness ran through her and she damned the man yet again. She wanted none of this. She tossed her head and quelled the unexpected sensations. 'No, thank you.'

He frowned at her curt tone, his back stiffening, his whole stance one of unconscious arrogance. 'I mean you no harm.' Evidently he was not accustomed to being refused.

She looked at him levelly, her eyes as blue as the sky above. 'I never for one moment thought you did.'

'Then why reject my offer?' he questioned abruptly. 'There are no more taxis. You'll have a long wait.'

'So,' she shrugged, 'I'll wait.' It would be infinitely preferable to subjecting herself to this man's practised charm. She was appalled that he had already found a chink in her armour and she was too weary to fight a verbal battle.

His lips twisted sardonically. 'A martyr, no less! Are you sure you won't change your mind?' His eyes flickered appraisingly over her, lingering indecently on the thrust of her breasts. Her thin cotton blouse was damp with perspiration and clung slavishly to her curves.

Kara's loins stirred and her hand tightened on her shoulder bag. His eyes rested momentarily on her wedding ring. 'But if that is your wish, then so be it,' he thrust, climbing abruptly into the waiting vehicle.

It was a further half-hour before a taxi returned, and Kara was fuming. If he had been a gentleman, a real gentleman, he would have let her have his.

And if she had any sense she would have accepted his offer, she told herself firmly. It had been ridiculous to refuse because he reminded her of her husband, because she had felt the same initial response as when she met Greg. Good lord, she was perfectly capable of handling herself now! She had learned the hard way what such men were like. Physically and sexually attractive themselves, they expected girls to fall at their feet like ninepins. Hmph! One such mistake was enough. No one would get near her again.

It was early evening when Kara finally reached Lakades, a beautiful island that from a distance looked like an emerald on a bed of blue velvet. She had pushed the irritating and disturbing stranger from her mind and was actually beginning to look forward to her holiday.

This time she found a taxi straight away. The island was tiny, two or three square miles, that was all, and the Tranakas vineyards cloaked nearly every square inch.

Sharon's employers, the Hythes, an English couple, worked for Tranakas Wines. Mr Hythe was undergoing an intensive two-year course prior to managing the UK operation. His wife worked part-time in the offices. They had tried a Greek nanny for their four-year-old twins, but it had not worked out, and Sharon had been delighted to get the job. In the twelve months her sister had been here she had frequently asked Kara to come out for a holiday, but she had always refused.

Her parents said she enjoyed being miserable, and perhaps they were right. She had been nowhere since Greg died because she was afraid of meeting someone else like him, someone who could hurt her. And seeing that man today told her she was right. He had brought back memories she would far rather forget, waking feelings she preferred to keep packed in ice.

They arrived, and Kara had been so deep in thought she had seen none of the island. She walked up the steps of a white villa set into the mountainside, casting her eyes over the gardens ablaze with exotic blooms, and waited for someone to answer her knock.

Below and all around, vineyards wove a green carpet,

and in the distance was the Ionian Sea. What an enchanting place! Perhaps she was worrying for nothing. Maybe a holiday here was the very antidote she needed.

A tall dark woman about the same age as herself answered the door. Her Twenties-style dress looked both cool and elegant.

'Mrs Hythe?'

The woman's smile was warm. 'That's right, and you must be Kara. Do come in.'

'It's very kind of you to let me stay here.' Kara followed her inside. How cool it was, and how welcome after the enveloping heat. 'But it wasn't necessary—I could easily have booked into a hotel.'

Rosemary Hythe laughed. 'You must be joking! Lakades is too small to boast a hotel. I hope you won't be bored—it's very quiet.'

'I don't think so,' smiled Kara. 'It's so beautiful.'

'Also lonely,' grimaced her hostess. 'Thank goodness for my job, that's what I say. I don't do much, mainly typing out Geoff's notes, but at least I meet people. I'll show you to your room. Sharon's taken Amanda and Damien for a walk. Normally they'd be in bed by now, but we promised they could stay up to meet you. By the time you've showered and changed they should be back.'

Kara followed her upstairs, their heels clicking in unison on the tiled treads.

'Here we are.' Rosemary stopped and opened a door. 'I do hope you'll be comfortable. This is the smallest room, but it has the nicest views.'

It was certainly tiny, but delightfully furnished in white and yellow, with sweet-smelling flowers in a vase on the dresser. Rosemary flung wide the shutters and revealed a breathtaking panorama of green-skirted

mountains and dusky valleys, of a dying sun and a
blood-red sea. On a distant peak were the pink-bathed
turrets of what looked like a fairy-tale palace.

Soon it would be dark. Already pinpoints of light were
appearing like glow-worms in the distance. 'It's out of
this world!' she breathed. 'What's that place? It looks
fantastic.'

Rosemary laughed. 'That's the Tranakas home. They
own virtually the whole island, this house included.' She
closed the shutters and drew white voile curtains before
switching on the light. 'The bathroom's next door.
Come down when you're ready.'

Kara did not linger. She unpacked and showered and
was down just as her sister walked through the door.
Sharon looked tanned and healthy and her hair, which
had always been lighter than Kara's, was bleached
almost white.

They did not look like sisters. Sharon was taller with a
good bone structure and classical features, whereas
Kara's face was delicate and elf-like with her hair
cropped correspondingly short.

'Kara!' beamed the younger girl. 'You're here!—and
you look so well, much better than when I left.'

'You look good too.' Kara took Sharon into her arms.
'Life out here obviously suits you.'

The twins were duly introduced, both with curly red
hair and laughing green eyes. They shook hands
seriously and complained loudly when Rosemary
ushered them to bed.

'You're very lucky, Sharon, to have found a job in a
place like this,' said Kara. 'It's heavenly.'

'It's not bad,' shrugged Sharon.

Something in her expression made Kara look at her
closely. 'You're not happy?'

'Of course I'm happy,' returned her sister sharply.

'But the twins are more of a handful than you expected? Is that it?'

'They're very high-spirited,' agreed Sharon. 'I'm sorry, Kara, I must take a shower before dinner. We ran all the way back and my clothes are sticking to me. '

Kara frowned, hoping Sharon wasn't being evasive. They had always been so close, always able to talk over each other's problems. Perhaps it was as well she had come. If something was worrying Sharon then she wanted to help.

Geoffrey Hythe turned out to be as friendly as his wife. He had sandy brown hair and a moustache, and was as thin as a lath.

'Sharon tells me you're taking over Tranakas Wines' UK operation?' said Kara.

'That's right,' he replied firmly. 'Up till now they haven't done very well in Britain, due mainly to lack of proper marketing. Aleko Tranakas intends to change all that.' He grinned approvingly.

Conversation naturally centred on the wine trade, and Kara was surprised how well informed her sister was. But she was disappointed when Sharon decided to go to bed early; she had hoped for a further word with her.

When Kara drew her curtains back the next morning she gasped her pleasure. The sky was pure azure and the hillsides as green and fresh as spring in England. Like Corfu, Lakades luxuriated in rain trapped by the mainland mountains of Greece. And what a difference it made!

From this angle the vines appeared to grow right to the water's edge, only an occasional red rooftop visible to indicate that there was other life—except for the Tranakas villa, of course. It stood tall and proud, and

Kara felt an urge to take a closer look.

She spent a delightfully lazy first day in the garden with her sister and the twins. The sun blazed out of a cloudless sky and a gentle breeze cooled them. She swam in the pool and sunbathed on the terrace, and they drank iced drinks and ate pomegranates and peaches straight from the tree. Sharon chatted incessantly about the twins and some of the antics they got up to, and she looked so happy and contented that Kara wondered whether she hadn't imagined something was wrong.

When Rosemary came home she announced that they had a guest for dinner. 'You'll like Aleko Tranakas,' she said. 'He's a super guy.'

Kara frowned. 'I don't think I should intrude. It's enough that you're letting me stay here.'

'Nonsense,' smiled Rosemary. 'Sharon always joins us, unless Amanda and Damien are being particularly troublesome.'

'Which isn't often,' put in Sharon. 'Once they're asleep we don't usually hear another peep out of them.'

'Looks as if I have no choice,' shrugged Kara. 'Exactly who is Aleko Tranakas?'

'Aleko,' said Rosemary with raised eyebrows, '*is* Tranakas Wines—make no mistake about that. The company was started by his father, but Aleko is now in complete control. Petros, his half-brother, who's only just into his twenties, is, much to his disgust, working his way up from the bottom. One day they'll be partners.'

'I see,' said Kara.

'I think Petros ought to be part of the management now,' said Sharon. 'It hardly seems fair.' There was a slight edge to her voice, causing Kara to look at her sharply.

'Petros knows nothing about the wine industry,' Rosemary reminded her, 'whereas Aleko was born into it.'

Sharon shrugged, looking faintly mutinous.

'Do you know Petros?' asked Kara, wondering why Sharon was defending him.

'I've met him a few times.' she admitted.

'He's been here with Aleko,' Rosemary explained. 'He's a nice enough boy but he hasn't the same confidence. Aleko's a born leader. He's full of ideas and has the ability to carry them through. Some people say he's too arrogant. He's aggressive, admittedly, but you don't get anywhere in business without that. I've always found him perfectly charming. Maybe it's because I'm a woman.'

'How old is he?' asked Kara.

'Mid-thirties, I imagine,' shrugged Rosemary.

'Is he married?'

'He hasn't had time, though he's never short of female company,' she added with a grin. 'If I were single I'd fancy him myself. But don't tell Geoff I said so!'

He sounded the type she hated most, and Kara suddenly wasn't sure whether she wanted to meet him. 'What do I wear?' she asked quietly.

'Something pretty. Aleko's always immaculate and he appreciates a woman dressing up.'

Kara caught Sharon's eye and knew her sister was aware of the thoughts running through her mind. But she couldn't avoid men for ever, could she?

She chose a pink silky strapless dress, the bodice and hemline delicately embroidered with silver thread and pearls. Not that she was dressing up to impress Aleko Tranakas, she told herself firmly. She wanted to impress no man. But she owed it to her hosts to look her best.

She applied the minimum of make-up and brushed her freshly washed hair until it shone. Unlike Sharon's heavy straight locks her hair had a tight natural curl and she kept it cropped short to keep it in place, not realising how much it suited her elfin-like features.

When she finally went downstairs the Hythes were sipping drinks in the lounge, everything was under control in the kitchen, and Aleko Tranakas had not yet arrived. Doors were open to the balcony where a bottle and glasses stood on a rattan table.

'I'm afraid Sharon won't be joining us,' said Rosemary. 'Damien's not feeling well.'

Kara frowned. 'It's nothing serious?'

The woman shook her head. 'You know what kids are like, up one minute, down the next. He probably had too much sun.'

Geoffrey Hythe poured a drink and handed it to Kara with a smile. 'Don't look so worried—it happens all the time. Tell me what you think of this.'

The wine was very dry and Kara shuddered as she took her first sip, but before she had chance to comment a white open-topped car screamed to a halt in the drive.

'Here's Aleko,' said Geoffrey. 'Bang on time as always. You could set your clock by him. He's never a minute late.'

Kara watched as the man, scorning the car door, vaulted over it and strode towards the house. He had the grace of a jungle animal: lithe, sensual, powerful—and she had seen him before!

Her pulses raced. It was inconceivable that this should be the same man she had spotted at the airport, the very same person who had offered to share his taxi. She could not drag her eyes away from him, and as he disappeared from view she turned towards the door and awaited him there. Even the Hythes were silent, as though a great presence was about to descend on them.

As he walked into the room his eyes rested momentarily on her, recognition in their dark depths, surprise too, and something more. Or had she imagined it? Was it what she expected and therefore read signals that were not there? Whatever, she could not ignore the sudden and painful beating of her heart, or the lump that had risen in her throat.

'Rosemary.' His attention was already on his hostess, and he took her hand, raising it gallantly to his lips. 'You look ravishing as always. Geoff's a lucky man.'

Faint colour tinged Rosemary's cheeks. 'So I keep telling him.'

'And Geoff, how are you? All is well, I hope?' He shook his employee's hand.

Kara watched him as though mesmerised. His English held barely an accent. His black trousers moulded a long length of tightly muscled thigh, his crisp white shirt was open at the neck to reveal the strong tanned column of his throat. There was a thrust to his jaw and the aggression Rosemary had spoken of was clearly visible, even though at this moment he was smiling. He was a man who could not be ignored, whatever the circumstances.

And then his eyes were upon her, coal-black and assessing, narrowed slightly, shadowed by thick brows, but missing nothing. 'So—we meet again. I hope you didn't have too long a wait?'

'Not at all,' she said, surprised to hear she sounded faintly breathless. Amazed, too, at the feelings he managed to arouse with one glance out of those smouldering black eyes. He had the knack of making a woman feel vulnerable, drawn to him against her will. His charisma was stronger even than Greg's had been. Oh God, please don't let it happen to me again, Kara prayed silently. I couldn't stand being hurt a second time.

'If I'd known this was your destination,' he was saying, 'I would have been more insistent about giving you a lift. You must have had a tedious journey?' His teeth were white and even and his smile all-encompassing.

'Yes, it is a pity, isn't it,' said Kara, but it was for the benefit of her hosts that she smiled sweetly. It would have been torture travelling in the company of this man, and certainly a hard-fought battle keeping him at bay. Even now, in front of these good people, he was doing nothing to hide his interest, and the damnable part of it was that she was responding.

Her whole body was a mass of sensation and she could imagine the heights to which he could send her. During the few months of her marriage she had discovered a sexuality in herself that she had never dreamt of, and although it had been kept under strict control since Greg's death there was no denying that here was a man who was capable of rekindling that fire.

'I wasn't aware that you'd met Kara?' Geoff's curiosity got the better of him.

'In Corfu, at the airport,' said Aleko pleasantly. 'But we haven't been formally introduced.'

'Then allow me,' said Geoff at once. 'Kara, this is Aleko Tranakas, the much-feared head of Tranakas Wines.'

Although this last was delivered with a smile Kara guessed there was more than a hint of truth in it. Despite his apparent friendliness Aleko gave the impression of being formidable. There was ruthlessness in the jut of his jaw, steel in the depth of his eyes, and an overall air of being in command. Always. Of his business, of his life, of his loves. His loves! Kara guessed he would be a dominant lover, an exciting one too, and she lowered her lids so that he should not read her thoughts.

'And Aleko, this is Kara Lincroft, Sharon's sister. She's here for a holiday.'

Kara took the outstretched hand—and felt as though she had touched a live wire. The charge of electricity that ran through her was unbelievable. What's happening to me? she asked herself. Why am I letting this man get through to me after all the vows I've made? It was incredible that she could react like this to a complete stranger. But you did to Greg, said a voice inside her. And look what happened, she told herself firmly. She clenched her teeth and tried to withdraw her hand—to no avail.

With a cynical smile he tightened his grip. 'Rosemary's mysterious guest? How pleased I am to make your acquaintance. And Mr Lincroft, where is he? How can he bear to let such an attractive wife out of his sight?'

His eyes locked into hers, telling her all too clearly that if she were his wife she would be kept closely shackled to his side. Telling her also that as she was here alone he considered her fair game. Kara smarted inside, and if it hadn't been for the Hythes she would have told him to mind his own business. Instead she announced quietly, 'I'm a widow.'

'So young?' His eyes widened. 'That's a pity. I'm truly sorry.'

Kara did not think so.

'This is the first holiday Kara has had since her husband died,' interjected Rosemary quietly, 'and

naturally we want to do all we can to make sure she
enjoys it.'

'Naturally.' Aleko lifted Kara's hand to his mouth,
pressing his lips against her soft skin, and lingering over-
long before giving it back to her. She felt as though she
was going to melt into the floor, and cursed herself for
being so weak.

'It would be my pleasure to provide some of your—
entertainment,' said Aleko quietly. 'In fact I would be
delighted to personally escort you on a tour of my
ambelon. You would enjoy seeing how the wines are
made, I am sure?'

'No, thank you,' replied Kara stiffly, anger with
herself making her voice tight. 'I've come to see my
sister. I intend spending most of my time with her.'

'But she is tied up with the twins. Surely there will be
occasions when you wish to be free of them, charming
though they are?' He sent a smile in Rosemary's
direction.

Kara wished he wasn't so persistent. What was it with
this man that he had to chat up every female he met? She
could not disregard the way he had worked at the
airport. But to do it so blatantly in front of his hosts was
unpardonable—and most embarrassing—and deeply
disturbing. Her heart had not beat so frantically in a long
time.

'I must go and see to the dinner,' apologised
Rosemary uneasily. She could sense the antagonism but
not guess the reason for it.

'And I'm forgetting my duty,' said Geoff. 'Your
wine, Aleko. Kara, would you like some more?'

'No, thanks,' she smiled, grateful for the diversion,
and picking up her glass took a long much-needed
swallow.

But she had forgotten how dry it was, and grimaced as the liquid reached her throat. Aleko was watching her.

'It is not to your taste?' His dark eyes were concentrating on her alone, telling her in no uncertain terms that he found her attractive, and that he would not give up easily.

She glanced anxiously at Geoff and found him watching her also. But his expression was one of amusement. He obviously knew how Aleko worked and was probably waging a bet with himself as to who would win.

'Something sweet, perhaps? Geoff, open a bottle of Muscat.'

Kara swallowed hard, accepting the wine when it was poured, treating Aleko to a cool disdainful smile. What an evening this promised to be! She had certainly never expected to meet a man who would instantly set her on fire. She had thought herself above such things, had learned the hard way how to control her emotions. What was going wrong?

This wine was much more palatable, and Kara finished the glass even before Rosemary invited them to take their places at the table. It helped calm her ragged nerves, and she hoped she was going to get through the evening without revealing to Aleko exactly the effect he had on her.

Conversation, as expected, was about wine and vineyards, about weather changes that could be detrimental to the crop, and the marvellous yield they'd had last year.

Kara would have let the conversation flow over her had Aleko not made sure she was never neglected, asking her opinion on one subject, or offering information about another. And always there was a message in his eyes. He was making it quite clear that he wanted to get to know her better.

Nor could she deny that her body was responding. He was a man no woman could resist—even Rosemary had admitted to being attracted, and she was happily married!

The way he held himself—as proud as a mountain lion; the way he gestured—fingers long and expressive; the way he spoke—with assurance and authority; they were all the marks of a man who knew exactly what his position in life was. He had reached the top and meant to stay there, and would climb even higher if it were humanly possible.

He was a bigger, more powerful version of Greg. And he was making a play for her the same as Greg had. Was it because she was tiny and looked fragile that men wanted to protect and cosset her? Or did they see a potential siren? Whatever, she had never invited their advances, and having been caught and hurt once she intended making doubly sure it didn't happen again. However hard it might be.

CHAPTER TWO

KARA was impatient for the meal to end. She found
Aleko's attention distinctly disturbing, all the more so
because of her unwitting response. The Hythes themselves seemed to find nothing untoward in his manner,
but had they any idea of the feverish emotions he was
arousing in her? She was appalled herself. How early,
she wondered, could she decently make her excuses and
go to her room? She must escape this man's suffocating
presence.

Her opportunity came when they moved back into the
living room for coffee and Aleko disappeared for a few
minutes. 'If you don't mind,' she said to Rosemary, 'I
think I'll go to bed—I'm very tired. It must be the
change of air. Thank you for the lovely meal.'

But at the bottom of the stairs she met Aleko. With an
inward groan she gave him a faint smile and a
murmured, 'Goodnight,' then ran quickly up.

'Kara!' His compelling voice halted her progress.

She turned and met the blackness of his eyes. 'Yes?' It
was a defiant yes.

'Come here.'

To her own amazement she slowly obeyed the
command, her legs moving against her will. Step by step
she descended until her eyes were on a level with his.

There were tiny lines about his eyes, almost invisible,
probably caused by squinting into the sun. His eyes
weren't black either, they were a very dark brown,
framed by long, thick lashes.

'What do you want?' she asked bluntly, almost

21

rudely, anxious only to go to her room. Her heart thumped frantically and painfully against her breast-bone and she could not imagine why he had called her back.

His hands came up and touched her face, gently, experimentally, his fingers reaching round to her nape, his thumbs stroking her chin. 'You intrigue me.'

His voice was deep and sexy, and her eyes widened and she jerked away, furious with herself for enjoying his touch. It was unbelievable that she did so, but it was true. Tiny quivers of excitement were darting through her body, awakening each and every one of the senses she had deliberately and firmly quelled.

He was the first man to touch her since Greg's death, she had managed to keep everyone else at bay, and the desire which exploded through her veins both alarmed and excited her. 'I can't think why,' she managed tightly, keeping her eyes averted from his far too perceptive gaze.

'You're trying very hard, I'll admit, but you're interested in me whether you like it or not.'

Her brows rose as she opened her mouth to protest at such outright conceit.

'Don't deny it,' he forestalled. 'What's wrong? Are you afraid that your sister might think you are betraying your husband's memory?'

'I hardly think so,' snapped Kara before she could stop herself.

His black brows rose at her caustic tone. 'It was not a happy marriage?'

'My private life is no business of yours.' Her voice was cool now, regretting her mistake, her chin high, and she strove hard for control.

'You're right, it isn't,' he agreed, 'but it's wrong to cut yourself off. Your sister has her commitments, whereas I can make myself at your disposal whenever you wish. Let me take you out, Kara. It would be my pleasure to show you our beautiful island.'

How easily words came to him! 'No, thanks,' she said acidly.

'I can't accept that you'd be happy spending your entire holiday with your sister and the twins. Amanda and Damien can be very tiresome.'

'You're not a child-lover?' she demanded, wishing he was not so persistent, even though the thought of his company was tempting. Her private vow to keep all men out of her life was dissolving fast.

He shrugged. 'I wouldn't say that, but it would be inexcusable to return to England without seeing anything of Lakades.'

'I think that's my problem.' Kara's eyes were bright. 'If I do decide to do some sightseeing, then rest assured I shan't be asking you to accompany me. Goodnight, Mr Tranakas.'

She spun round, but he leapt up the stairs and was ahead of her. 'That's quite a sizeable chip you have on your shoulders, Kara. What type of a man was he that did this to you?' His eyes narrowed into dark slits, and he looked as though he would not move until she gave him a satisfactory answer.

What would he say, she wondered, if she revealed that Greg had been a very similar person to himself? Smooth-tongued and persuasive, physically very attractive, mentally stimulating—a powerful combination and not one many women could resist. She had fallen heavily and was still picking up the pieces.

'He was not what he appeared on the surface,' she said quietly, 'and that's all I'm prepared to tell you. May I go now?' Her eyes were on a level with his waist and she had to throw back her head to look at him.

He shrugged. 'I'm not stopping you.'

But she did have to climb past him! Her heart pounded uncomfortably as she mounted the two steps that brought her to his level. One more and their eyes were parallel. She ought to have hurried on upwards instead of stopping. It was a big mistake.

His arms snaked behind her and the next moment his mouth was on hers, his hard body crushing the breath out of her. Sensations rippled through her like the wind through a tree, and she could no more reject him that she could stop the forces of nature itself.

It was not a brutal kiss, it was sensual. It was exploratory and persuasive, physically exciting, and when he put her from him Kara took a while to come to her senses. By this time he had left her side and descended to the bottom of the stairs.

'Goodnight, my beautiful Kara,' he whispered. 'Tomorrow we shall meet again.' And before she could reply he disappeared.

Anger quickly took the place of pleasure and she marched stiffly up to her room, her cheeks flushed, her head high. How dared he assume that one kiss was all it took to make her change her mind! What an arrogant, self-opinionated man he was!

It had been a shattering kiss, admittedly, and she had reacted far more strongly than she had ever imagined possible, but that was the beginning and end of the relationship so far as she was concerned.

She took a much-needed cool shower and then went in search of her sister. It was pointless going to bed yet; Aleko had dashed all hopes of sleep.

Sharon was in the twins' bedroom, sitting on a chair beside Damien's bed, his hand held in hers.

'How is he?' whispered Kara.

'Asleep now and much better, I think.' Sharon

carefully slid her hand from his. 'Lord, I'm stiff! Did you want me for anything special?'

'Just to chat,' said Kara, following Sharon into her room next door. 'We haven't really had any time alone.'

'Has Aleko gone? He doesn't normally leave this early.' Sharon yawned and stretched and stripped off her dress before throwing herself down on the bed.

'I don't think so.'

Her brows rose. 'You left the party early?'

'I wish you'd been there.' Kara perched on the end of the bed and eyed her sister ruefully. 'I found Aleko more than a little overpowering.'

Sharon laughed. 'Rosemary did warn you.'

'I know, but I never dreamt he'd home in on me so quickly.'

'I heard you on the stairs,' admitted Sharon. 'It's a pity you're against him. It's time you started dating again. You can't go on for ever shutting men out of your life.'

'Maybe,' snorted Kara, 'but I saw him at Corfu airport chatting up a girl, and I'd previously spotted him at Heathrow doing exactly the same thing. A bit of a coincidence, you might think, but it's a fact. He's a slimy snake and I hate him. I don't want to talk about him.' Or was it her own feelings she did not want to talk about? Her skin prickled with heat each time she recalled that kiss. It was a damnable state of affairs.

'Tell me about you,' she said to Sharon conversationally, still more than a little concerned about her sister, even though Aleko had temporarily driven all such thoughts from her mind. 'I remember in one of your letters you said you'd met some fabulous boy. Are you still seeing him?'

Sharon's face went blank and she turned her head away.

'Okay, I won't pry,' said Kara quickly. It looked as though the romance was going through a sticky patch. All she could do was wait for Sharon to tell her in her own good time. 'When's your next day off?' she asked, changing her tone. 'I don't fancy exploring by myself.'

'I only have one weekend in four and the half days when Rosemary's not working,' said Sharon apologetically.

Kara frowned. 'But surely while I'm here she'll give you more free time?'

'No, she won't,' cried Sharon.

Feeling mystified, Kara said, 'I can't understand why you're so certain. How about if I ask her? I'm sure she won't object.'

'I'd rather you didn't,' said Sharon, facing her sister at last, her eyes oddly disturbed. 'We could take Amanda and Damien with us, if you like. They'll love it.'

Kara shrugged. It seemed strange to her that Sharon did not want to ask for time off. Unless she had abused the woman's generosity in the past—when she was going out with that boy, maybe?

'If you don't mind, Kara,' said Sharon, getting up suddenly, 'I'd like to go to bed. I might be woken up in the night, so I must snatch an hour or two while I can.'

'Of course,' said Kara quietly. She stood up too and gave her sister a swift hug. 'If there's something bothering you, Sharon, something you'd like to talk about, please feel free. We never used to have any secrets. We——'

'Why should there be?' snapped Sharon, shrugging away.

'No reason.' said Kara softly. 'I just—oh well, never mind. Goodnight, Sharon, I'll see you tomorrow.'

Her sister's emphatic denial spoke for itself. Perhaps she was still madly in love and the boy wanted nothing more to do with her? It hurt that she would not confide. It was unlike Sharon to keep things to herself.

But then being in love did strange things to people. It had to her. She had known Greg was a womaniser when she met him but would listen to no words of warning. He had said she was the girl he had been looking for all his life, and naïvely she had believed him.

She went back to her room, wishing Sharon would not bottle things up. A problem shared was a problem halved, so the saying went. But it was early days. Perhaps by the end of her holiday Sharon would be prepared to discuss this boy who was making her unhappy.

The next morning Damien had a temperature, and a doctor was sent for from the mainland. Kara was surprised to discover there were no doctors on Lakades, and she wondered what happened when an emergency arose. Rosemary stayed at home and Kara knew there was no chance of a private conversation with her sister. There was nothing for it but to go exploring on her own.

With no real idea of where she was going Kara left the house and trudged down the hill. She bade good morning to an old woman in a voluminous black dress who was leading a donkey overladen with hay. She admired unexpected vistas of shiny blue sea and neat little coves, and smelled the delicious aroma from orange and lemon trees. But most impressive of all was the serried ranks of vines. In whatever direction she looked they stretched as far as the eye could see. And they all belonged to Aleko Tranakas!

He had said, she remembered, that he would see her today. Worrying about Sharon she had almost forgotten his strange statement. It was as well she had left the house; she did not want to be there if he came looking for her.

The village at the bottom of the hill was no more than

a narrow street with a few scattered houses. Men sat
outside the taverna, glasses of beer on the tables in front
of them, nodding a greeting, their eyes frankly
admiring.

Finally Kara found a tiny cove, the sea so clear and
sparkling with sunlight that it dazzled her eyes. How she
wished she had come prepared for a swim. She sat for a
while and watched some children splashing in the
shallows, then walked on further along the coast.

It was nearing lunchtime now, and she felt hot and
hungry as well as being tired and wished she had not
wandered so far. Apart from the village she had seen no
other houses or shops. There was nothing for it but to
make her way back.

She saw the car coming towards her, but not until it
stopped did she recognise it as Aleko's. Her heart
stopped beating as her eyes met his, and she felt again
that irrational response. What madness was taking her
over?

'Jump in,' he said cheerfully, his teeth very white
against the polished tan of his skin. 'I hoped I might find
you and persuade you to join me for lunch. Rosemary
said you'd gone walking. I've just been to pick up some
papers I left Geoff to look through.'

'Really?' Kara did not bother to hide her scepticism.
'If they're that important wouldn't he have taken them
to the office this morning?' It was a feeble excuse. Did
he expect her to believe it?

'It was the idea,' he said. 'But the poor man's so
worried about his son that he forgot.'

And Aleko himself had come to fetch them! Not
Geoff, who would have been the obvious person, since it
gave him the opportunity to check on his son.

She looked at him scornfully. He wore lightweight
grey trousers and a white shirt, the jacket to his suit lying

on the back seat. He looked cool and relaxed, and Kara felt hot and irritable. She had wanted to avoid him, but he had found her, and she did not know how to get out of the situation.

'I'm not hungry,' she tried.

'You've already eaten?'

'No, but——'

'Then you have no excuse.' He leaned across and opened the door. 'Get in. I know a delightful little taverna where the food cannnot be faulted.'

Reluctantly she joined him, and it was in fact a relief to sit down, even though his nearness set her pulses racing at twice their normal speed. She could smell the same spicy woody scent that had lingered in her nostrils last night, and she knew that even when this holiday was over it would still remind her of him.

Aleko set the car in motion, and when the breeze lifted her hair and cooled her face she felt a whole lot better. Had it been anyone else beside her other than this overpoweringly sexual man she would have enjoyed her ride up the mountain. As it was, she was scared of her reaction.

'It was a little foolish walking so far without a hat, and without food inside you.' He lifted his brows as he glanced across. 'It's a good job I spotted you. You looked all in.'

Kara threw him a disdainful glance. 'I didn't need you. I'm fine.'

'I'm glad to hear it,' he said politely. 'But just in case you consider doing the same thing again I should warn you that tavernas are few and far between on Lakades. We don't cater for tourists, so it's unwise to walk too far unprepared.'

'Thanks for the warning,' she said primly. 'I'll remember next time.'

'As I said last night, I'm quite prepared to be your guide. It can't be any fun wandering around on your own.'

His dark eyes slanted suggestively over her, and Kara felt an impossible heat pervade her body. He was right, but even so her own company was infinitely preferable to his. He was making it perfectly clear what he was after—and she was finished with men for all time. 'And as *I* said last night, thanks for the offer, but no.'

His lips compressed and the car surged forward. In a matter of minutes they had reached a remote village perched on the mountainside.

The taverna was a tiny one-storied building with whitewashed walls and green wooden shutters. A wide portico shaded the front, a Virginia creeper climbing up its supports, and they sat at a table covered by a green and white check plastic cloth. The whole effect was cool and relaxing and encouraged Kara to forget her antagonism.

There were no other customers and the owner, a bald-headed man with an unusually large moustache, greeted them as though they were long-lost friends.

Kara let Aleko choose for her, and while the two men discussed the menu she admired the colourful garden with its bright red geraniums and golden sunflowers. It was odd seeing familiar English flowers growing side by side with exotic blooms whose names she did not know.

Far below the Ionian Sea sparkled and danced and all about them birds and butterflies went about their daily work. It was impossible not to be affected by her surroundings.

'I like it here,' she said impulsively. 'It's beautiful, like being in a world of your own.'

His smile encompassed her. 'It has that effect. But the

best is yet to come. Yanni's cooking is a treat not to be missed.'

And he wasn't exaggerating. Yanni's *stiphades*, meat baked in the oven with onions and tomato sauce, was delicious. Kara could have eaten it again. They washed it down with a wine which Aleko assured her was not one of his own, and his behaviour was impeccable.

He kept her entertained with stories about the islands and she almost forgot that he had been making advances to her last night, though it was not so easy to dismiss her own awareness.

'I think we should go,' he said at length, his lips quirking when she pulled a rueful face. 'You're enjoying it here?'

She nodded. 'Very much so.'

'Good,' he smiled. 'I am glad you feel that way. It is wrong that you should curl up inside your shell. You should never let one bad experience prejudice you for the rest of your life.'

They wound down the mountain, Aleko silent now as he concentrated on the tortuous hairpin bends, Kara busy with her thoughts. He was right, of course, but how did she know who she could trust? Men were so adept at turning on the charm. Who could tell when they were sincere?

She had firmly believed that Greg loved her. Perhaps he had, in his own way—but that still did not stop him having affairs with other women. Were all men the same, some more clever than others so that they were never found out? Aleko was a charmer, he would certainly never be content with one woman alone. It would be insanity getting involved, even though her body at this very moment was calling out for fulfilment. For two years she had denied herself any sexual enjoyment, and this was why she reacted so strongly now.

She determinedly concentrated on the changing scenery. On the higher slopes the vines had given way to olives, gnarled and twisted trees that looked as though they had grown there for ever.

At one particular spot Aleko stopped the car and they got out, and the views were out of this world. The ground dropped away beneath them, olives and the occasional cypress closely clothing the slopes. Beyond came the inevitable vineyards, from this distance nothing more than a verdant carpet. And finally the ocean, a brilliant, dazzling peacock blue.

There was no sound to be heard except those of nature. A faint rustle as the breeze stirred the silvery leaves of the olives, the call of an invisible bird, the distant bleat of a goat. No traffic noise, no pollution. Just a faint fragrance borne on the currents of air.

'It's beautiful, Aleko,' said Kara softly.

'Yes, isn't it.'

She inhaled appreciatively and turned to him, her smile fading when she discovered he was looking at her and not the fantastic panorama. Nor was it a casual glance, there was a whole depth of meaning in his eyes. He was spoiling what had promised to be an enjoyable few hours.

She tried to laugh. 'I meant the view.'

'So did I. I'm glad you're relaxing, Kara.' He brushed his fingers against her cheek. 'You're very beautiful when you're not on the defensive.'

His touch, though light as a butterfly's wing, felt like a branding iron, and she swung away, closing her eyes, trying her hardest to quell the sudden quickening of her pulses. 'Flattery won't get you anywhere,' she said, her voice husky with suppressed emotion. Years ago she had fallen for every line that was spun her, but not any more.

'I mean it.' He rested his hand on her shoulder and turned her to face him.

Kara's stomach churned. What an exciting male animal he was! How long could she continue to hold out against him?

'You're wrong to shut men out of your life completely, Kara. You're a very sensual woman. Why not stop fighting the inevitable?'

She flashed her blue eyes. 'Inevitable? I see nothing inevitable about having an affair with you.' God, what a lie that was! If he continued to persist it was as inevitable as summer following spring. Her resistance was falling by the second.

'You don't?' His heavy brows rose, his eyes wide, the whites very white against the blackness of his irises. 'In that case perhaps a little of your English strategy is called for?' His lips curved into a secretive smile, his eyes narrowing so that she could no longer see their expression.

Kara frowned uneasily. 'I don't know what you're talking about.'

'Actions speak louder than words, isn't that right?'

'It is one of our sayings, yes, but——'

She got no further. His arms imprisoned her, his lips cut off her protest. Feelings she had tried so hard to stem this last hour broke free, filling her limbs with tingling sensation. An involuntary whimper escaped the back of her throat. How she had missed a man's touch, a man's love! She had starved herself without realising it, and now the floodgates were open and she was unable to suppress the rising tide of her emotion.

Nevertheless she knew the insanity of allowing such a situation, and a few seconds' pleasure was all she allowed herself before she fought fiercely to escape.

'Get your hands off me, Aleko!' Desperately she twisted her head from side to side, trying to push herself away, pitting her strength against his.

He held her at arm's length, a tiny puzzled frown creasing his brow. 'Don't fight me, Kara,' he muttered.

'Don't fight, when you're kissing me against my will?' she demanded heatedly. Against her will? Against her better judgement? Yes. But against the hunger of her body, no. She was spiting herself.

'But it need not be. You think I don't know that deep down inside you crave fulfilment? A woman is made to be loved, Kara. Don't fight what is right and natural.'

She shook her head wildly. 'I've finished with all that. I've had my trust in the male sex totally destroyed. You're all the same, hot-blooded and lustful. All you want is a woman's body, you don't give a damn for her emotions!'

Kara was furiously angry. With herself for weakening, for feeling as lustful as she had accused him of being. And with Aleko for being able to do this to her. For being so persistent, for demonstrating so tantalisingly what a good lover he could be.

His hands dropped to his sides. 'Do I take it that you plan to shut men out of your life for ever?'

'I might do. It depends.'

'On what?'

'Whether I meet a man I can trust.'

His nostrils flared. 'You've already formed an opinion about me?'

She nodded.

'Thanks for the vote of confidence,' he snarled, 'though I fail to see how you can reach a decision when you refuse to give yourself time to get to know me.' He turned away and climbed back into his car and the journey to the Hythes' was accomplished in seething silence.

Kara went into the house without a backward glance, and bumped immediately into Sharon outside Damien's room.

'How is he?' she asked at once.

'Much better,' replied her sister. 'His temperature's already dropping. The doctor says he's probably picked up a virus and that he'll be as right as rain in forty-eight hours.'

'That's good,' smiled Kara. 'I'll go into him in a little while. I want to shower and change first. Where's Amanda?' It was strange not hearing their happy voices.

'Rosemary's taken her to the beach. She kept running in and out and I was having the devil's own job keeping Damien in bed. It's a wonder you didn't see them. I thought you went that way?'

Kara pulled a wry face. 'I met Aleko. He bought me lunch.'

Sharon's lovely eyes widened. 'You're friends now?'

'Not likely,' thrust Kara strongly. 'I don't want a two-week affair, which is all he's after.'

Sharon looked at her thoughtfully. 'But you are ready to start going out with men again?'

'What makes you think that?'

'Well, you're not entirely averse to him, I can tell. It's just that he reminds you of Greg. Not that I think he does—they're poles apart. Aleko's a real dishy man.'

'You sound as though you fancy him yourself?'

Sharon wrinkled her nose in distaste and shook her head.

'But there is someone you're interested in?' Kara pressed home her advantage.

Her sister shrugged. 'There might be. Isn't that Damien? I must go.'

Kara had heard nothing and she felt acutely disappointed in Sharon. It was becoming clear that her sister wanted to avoid being alone with her. And probably this was the reason she had said Rosemary would give her no time off.

She went to her room, her mood thoughtful, and when she joined Sharon and Damien after her shower she was determined not to be put off again.

But the little boy was enjoying being the centre of attention and never stopped talking. And when Amanda came back, full of tales about how far she had swum, there was no chance at all.

Nor did Sharon join the Hythes and herself for dinner. Rosemary said she had already eaten, but Kara had her doubts.

It inevitably happened that Amanda caught Damien's virus, and for the next few days Kara saw hardly anything of Sharon. She spent most of her time by the pool acquiring a tan, afraid to go and explore in case she bumped into Aleko. She had never expected to feel chemically attracted to any man again, and it was her bad luck that she had chosen a womaniser like Aleko to waken her dormant desires.

'Why don't you take Kara and show her around the vineyard?' suggested Rosemary Hythe to her husband one evening. 'I'm sure she'd enjoy it.'

He looked at Kara, his thin sandy brows raised questioningly.

'Aleko's already asked me,' she said with a faint smile. 'And I refused.'

'You don't like the idea?'

Kara grimaced. 'It's not that, it's Aleko. I—I don't really like him. And it could prove embarrassing if we bump into each other,' she finished faintly.

'You surprise me,' said Rosemary. 'Most women

swoon at the sight of him.'

'He reminds me of my husband. From a distance it could even be him,' explained Kara, wishing the woman wouldn't keep singing his praises. Didn't she know that he was a type not to be trusted? That he would never be true to one woman and all he was after was sex?

'And that's a bad thing?' queried Geoff.

She nodded. 'He wasn't a very—good husband.'

'Oh, I'm sorry,' said Rosemary at once. 'I honestly didn't know.'

Kara closed her eyes momentarily. 'It was a long time ago, and I should be over him. My parents can't understand why I'm still hurt and won't go out and enjoy myself. It was only at their insistence that I'm here now.'

'And I ruined things by inviting Aleko,' commented Rosemary ruefully. 'What can I say?'

'Nothing,' said Kara firmly. 'You weren't to know.'

'He won't be at the vineyard tomorrow,' announced Geoff unexpectedly. 'He's off to Athens for a couple of days.'

Kara grinned. 'In that case, I accept. I'd really like to see how wine is made.'

On their drive to the *ambelon* the next morning Geoff pointed out an ancient disused monastery, and the tiny cemetery on top of a hill. There were no other villages, just a few scattered houses and an occasional old woman or a black-robed, white-bearded priest making their way slowly along the steep roads.

He also told her a little about the Tranakas vineyards which covered so much of the island. 'Soil and climate are the two most important factors in determining the quality of wine,' he informed her. 'Therefore a different type of grape is grown on the more sheltered eastern side of the island from that on the exposed west coast.'

'I see,' she said, musing on what her feelings would be

if it were Aleko beside her. She would definitely not be sitting so comfortably. Her heart would race and she would feel the awareness that was becoming an integral part of her when he was around. It was a relief that he had kept out of her way these last few days. Perhaps he had accepted that she really did want nothing to do with him?

'—and these light wines don't travel well, so unfortunately we cannot export them.'

Kara murmured something non-committal, wondering how much she had missed. But Geoff was back on his favourite topic again and did not seem to notice that she was not listening.

When a huddle of white buildings came into sight she knew they were nearly there, and she sat forward, her eyes now wide with interest.

They drove beneath an arch with the name Tranakas in big black iron letters over the top, and once he had parked the car they strode together towards the office block.

It was a shock when the first person they met was Aleko. Kara's mouth fell open and her heart skidded to an abrupt halt. Geoff must have been mistaken, he wasn't in Athens after all. How she wished she could make herself invisible!

As usual, he was immaculately dressed in lightweight slack sand a pristine white shirt, and he looked arrogantly, disturbingly handsome. She feasted her eyes on him hungrily, her senses immediately re-awakened, asking herself what power he wielded that could do this to her.

His smile encompassed them both, but it was on her that his eyes fell. 'Good morning, Kara, Geoff. What a delightful surprise.'

Geoff gave a nervous cough. 'Good morning, Aleko. I've persuaded Kara to come and have a look around. It would be criminal if she went back without seeing your set-up.'

'Absolutely,' agreed Aleko.

'I hope you don't mind?'

'Not in the least.' His smile was disarming, no hint at all of the circumstances in which they had last parted. 'How are you enjoying your holiday, Kara? Getting out and about, I hope?'

'No she's not,' answered Geoff, much to her annoyance. 'With the twins ill, Sharon's been too busy to show her around.'

'That is a pity.' Aleko fixed his dark eyes upon her. 'Why didn't you give me a call?'

It sounded an innocent enough question and Geoff looked expectantly at her, giving an apologetic shrug when he saw her compressed lips and the fierce frown creasing her brow.

'You already know how I feel about that,' said Kara quietly.

'And it is why you deliberately chose a day to come here when you thought I'd be out?' Aleko's eyes narrowed. 'I'm sorry to disappoint you, Kara. My trip was cancelled at the last minute.'

She lifted her shoulders, 'How unfortunate,' and turned to Geoff. 'Are you ready?'

He looked acutely embarrassed, but Kara had no qualms at all about insulting Aleko. He knew exactly how she felt about him.

Footsteps behind made them turn. A young man approached Geoff. 'I've been looking for you. Stavros wants to know whether you're ready.'

'Ready?' Geoff frowned and then clapped a hand to his brow. 'Oh, lord, I'd forgotten! I'm supposed to be going with him to look at those vines which have been attacked by that mystery bug.' Then his face cleared. 'But never mind, you can come with us, Kara. We'll start your tour there.'

'I have a better idea.'

They both looked at Aleko.

His eyes were intent upon Kara. 'I will take you.'

'But——' began Geoff.

'No arguments,' said Aleko firmly.

Geoff gave Kara a rueful glance. There was nothing more he could say. Aleko had made up his mind.

She shrugged and gave in, but more because she did not want to embarrass Geoff further than because she was afraid to defy Aleko. The tour shouldn't take long, an hour at the most—she could surely survive that? Then she would ask him to take her back to the Hythes'. She would give him no opportunity to make any sexual advances.

But when Aleko tucked his hand beneath her elbow all hell broke loose inside her, and it took all her self-control to let none of it show. 'We'll go to my office,' he said. 'I have a few papers to sort out first.'

There was a triumphant gleam in his eyes, and Kara cursed whatever fate had thrown them together. It already looked as though it might not be so easy to hold him off as she had hoped.

CHAPTER THREE

ALEKO'S office was like any other executive suite: stylish, immense and luxuriously furnished. He seated Kara in a leather armchair, his eyes on hers for several heart-stopping seconds before he crossed to his desk and began to systematically go through a pile of papers.

Totally engrossed in what he was doing, he seemed to have forgotten her presence, but Kara could not dismiss him so easily, and she took the opportunity to study his darkly handsome features.

Not that she needed to; she could shut her eyes and conjure up his image any time. But it felt good sitting looking at him. She had an urge to run her fingers through the rich blackness of his hair, trace a line down that autocratic nose, outline the shape of his mouth. His hands too excited her—tanned and lean, his fingers long, the nails immaculate. She could feel them on her, exploring her—as she wanted to touch him!

Her adrenalin flowed and with a hint of anger at herself for being so foolish she pushed herself up and walked over to the window. She looked out at the white buildings and scurrying men, wondering whether it was fear of Aleko that made them hurry or whether they enjoyed what they were doing.

When she turned round he was watching her, and looked as though he had been for some time. His long legs were stretched out in front of him, the fine material of his trousers taut across muscular thighs.

There was a secret smile on his lips and his eyes were

narrowed, but she could guess what he was thinking. He wanted her as much as she, at this moment, wanted him. His whole presence filled the room. She could not escape him. He did not have to touch her to make her aware of him. Who had she been fooling when she thought she could go on this tour and escape with her feelings intact?

'Have you finished?' she asked, her husky tone giving away the fact that she was emotionally disturbed. Heavens, her heart was going like a traction engine!

'My paperwork? Yes.' He smiled knowingly and pushing himself up came over to her.

Kara backed against the window, her fingers gripping the sill. If she was not careful Aleko would hear her heart beating. Did he have to stand so close? Why had she let herself get into this situation? Why hadn't she been firm and gone along with Geoff instead?

'Then I think we ought to get this tour over and done with as quickly as possible,' she said. 'I'm sure you must have other things to do without wasting your time on me.'

'My work for the day is finished,' he announced smilingly. 'I had planned to be in Athens, don't forget. I'm yours for as long as you care to put up with me.'

Kara held his gaze for a couple of seconds. What a tantalising thought that was! Then, aghast at her own wantonness, she turned away, wishing he would move also. He was close, much too close for comfort, even though he made no attempt to touch her. She was weakening, she was weakening quickly. He was making her realise what she had done to herself these last years. Her pent-up emotions were increased tenfold now they were being finally released.

'What's wrong, Kara?' he mocked softly. 'Are you afraid of your own response to me?'

She did not answer, keeping her eyes downcast. He made her feel self-conscious and foolish, like a schoolgirl on the threshold of first love. Were her feelings so obvious?

'I'm not going to touch you, Kara, not unless it's what you want. On the other hand, I might as well tell you that you do the same to me.' And to prove his words he took her hand and placed it on his chest. His heart thudded as erratically as her own.

She looked at him and smiled ruefully, and he laughed and held her to him for a second, that was all. 'Let's go,' he said gruffly, 'before I make a liar of myself and break my word.'

Kara felt suddenly and surprisingly happy. Aleko had just proved that he put her feelings before his own. Whereas Greg had rushed her headlong into an affair and marriage this man was quite prepared to slow the pace to suit her, even though their time together was short. Maybe she had misjudged him. Or was it that his methods were more subtle? He knew how she felt and realised he would get nowhere if he rushed her. Was that it?

She shrugged mentally. Whatever, there was no sense in ruining her holiday. He had given his word and somehow she knew that he meant it. It was up to her now. If she wanted to hold him off for the rest of the time she spent here then she could do so, and enjoy his company at the same time.

They left the office block and she walked silently at his side until they reached the first of the buildings. Annoyingly she found it more difficult than ever to ignore his sexuality. The fact that he had promised to leave her strictly alone had the adverse effect of inciting her to fever-pitch.

He pointed out the huge crushers which at this moment were lying idle. 'It's essential,' he said, 'that grapes are picked at exactly the right moment and taken quickly to be crushed.'

She listened to the deeply resonant tones of his voice. 'This is especially important where white grapes are concerned, otherwise oxidization takes place and spoils the colour and quality of the wine.'

How sexy he was! Kara hadn't realised before. Aleko clearly loved his work and spoke of the process with pride and reverence, but she could also imagine that same voice uttering words of love. A shiver rode down her spine.

'If we're producing white wine we separate the stalks, skin and pips before the first stage of fermentation; with red we leave them in. At this part of the operation the wine is called must.'

They were moving slowly towards the huge fermentation vats, though Kara was more aware of Aleko than the vats themselves. He smiled down at her and it was as though they were building up a mental rapport. It was astonishing how quickly her hostility had faded. And all because he had promised not to touch her!

She felt safe now. Safe to admit the feelings that warmed her, safe to indulge in her private fantasies. And she could not help wondering what kind of a lover he would make. He would be considerate, that was for sure—never impatient, letting her dictate the pace. All this she had learned in the last few minutes. An affair with Aleko would be one to remember with pleasure, not pain.

As he went into detail of the fermentation process she tried her hardest to listen, but it was difficult—with her mind on other things.

'Afterwards,' he continued, 'the wine is clarified and perhaps blended with another one before being filtered and poured into barrels for maturing. Are you listening, Kara?'

She nodded, unaware of the brilliance in her eyes. 'Yes, of course. It's fascinating.'

He gave a satisfied smile, and they made their way into the cellars where row upon row of barrels created an impressive array. His arm brushed hers and she drew in a swift breath. Contact with him was explosive, like nothing she had ever felt before. She could not help wondering whether he was deliberately making his tone sensual, whether the way he kept glancing at her wasn't designed to set her pulses racing a little bit faster.

His commentary continued. 'From time to time the wine is racked—that means it is transferred into fresh barrels to remove any sediment.'

Kara nodded, doing her best to look as though she was taking it all in.

'The wine is matured for a minimum of two years,' he informed her, 'a lot longer for the better ones. If necessary, after testing, they are further treated or blended, then filtered again, bottled and corked. Can you follow that? Am I going too quickly?'

'It's perfectly clear,' she replied, aware that she was smiling foolishly.

'Some wines also spend time ageing in the bottles. And you might hear of wine producers who freeze their wine before bottling. Some never age it in the bottles at all. It varies widely.'

His enthusiasm and knowledge came across strongly, and Kara began to feel guilty that she was paying more attention to Aleko himself rather than his explanation of the varying processes.

'And that's about it,' he said, finally leading the way outside into the warm sunshine.

It was over so quickly. Kara felt sad. He would take her home now and she had so enjoyed this last half hour, more than she would ever admit.

He glanced down at her crestfallen face. 'You look sorry?'

'I suppose I am,' she confessed carefully. 'I'm not much of a wine drinker, but I found it all extremely interesting. I never realised exactly how much work is involved.'

'And I thought you weren't listening,' he mocked. 'Perhaps, while we're such—good friends, I might suggest a tour of the island? We grow several different types of grape, each dependent on its separate location.'

Kara smiled, feeling suddenly happy again. 'Yes, I know, Geoff told me.'

'So you will come?'

She nodded.

He looked pleased too and led her to his waiting jeep. It was ideal for this mountainous island, and in whichever direction he drove vineyards cascaded down hillsides like rushing green seas.

She caught glimpses of women in full skirts and ill-fitting blouses working their small squares of land. Everyone knew Aleko, waving and smiling, calling a greeting, glancing curiously at his companion.

'Enjoying it?' he asked, grinning as she clung on for dear life when he swung round a particularly sharp bend.

'Very much.' And this was the truth. His behaviour was as exemplary as he had promised it would be, and it was the first time Kara had relaxed in a man's company since Greg died. If relaxed was the appropriate word.

She was too aware of him, really, for her own peace of mind. Her whole body pulsed with desire, sensations spinning through her limbs like a rocket out of control.

She caught glimpses of an impossibly blue sea and tiny inviting coves. There were pink and white villas set into pockets of land on the hillsides, and it was all so beautiful that she felt sad it would all too soon be no more than a memory.

Aleko pointed out the different varieties of grape and she wondered how he remembered them all. 'It sounds very confusing to me,' she laughed.

'In which case I will feed you no more information,' he told her. 'I want you to retain clear memories, not a jumble of facts and figures that mean nothing.'

Kara smiled. 'I shall always remember today.'

His brows rose. 'If that's a compliment, thank you. Would it have been so enjoyable if Geoff had escorted you?'

It was a leading question and Kara thought carefully before answering. She had already given too much away. 'I don't think so. Wine-making is in your blood. Geoff is only learning. Your enthusiasm is infectious.'

'I'm very proud of what we do here,' he agreed. 'Of course our wine output is negligible compared with countries like France and Italy. We've never really had a good reputation. I think we were judged by our Retsina, which is raw by anyone's standards, but it's a growing industry and I want the name Tranakas to be up with the best.'

'I hope you succeed, I really do,' she said fervently.

He smiled. 'Thank you. That's the nicest thing you've said to me yet. I must be making progress.'

Kara did not answer. He was progressing by leaps and bounds, if only he knew it.

Aleko drew the jeep to a halt and turned in his seat towards her. 'But if I'm to get anywhere at all with you I need to know about that husband of yours.'

Kara stiffened. 'No! It's nothing at all to do with you. I——'

'Kara,' he said gently, 'you're letting him ruin your life. Because of him you're denying yourself the pleasures of your body. It is a woman's right. She is made to be loved and pampered and cherished, to feel the most wanted and the most beautiful person in the world. And you are beautiful, also very sensual, and it's criminal that you should suppress your emotions in this way.'

'Is all this supposed to make me say yes to you?' she demanded. 'Is flattery supposed to get you anywhere?' Oh God, how she wanted him, but was it wise to give way to her desires for a few days' sexual pleasure? He was trying hard, she had to admit. It must be a change for him not to have his female companion falling at his feet.

He shook his head. 'I've told you, I won't touch you unless you want it too. But I don't want you to destroy yourself. Already, today, I can see a change in you, and I hope I can take the credit for it, but until you exorcise your husband's ghost you'll never truly be able to enjoy life as you should.'

'It's my life,' she shrugged. 'Why should it matter to you?'

He looked at her solemnly. 'Because I—like you, Kara. And as I said to you before, you intrigue me. You also once hinted that I was the same type of man as your husband.' His lips tightened momentarily. 'I cannot see myself hurting a woman as you have been hurt. Don't you think you owe me an explanation?'

Kara sighed. What harm would it do? And maybe he

was right, maybe she did need to talk to someone about Greg. 'I loved him very much,' she said quietly. 'He was my whole life.' A lump rose in her throat. 'When I discovered that he'd been unfaithful to me, not once, but repeatedly, I wanted to die.'

Aleko frowned. 'And that's how you see me—a good-time guy? Unable to ever remain true to one woman?'

His tone was harsh and she could see that she had angered him. But how did she know it was not true? It was easy to put on an act—if you wanted something badly enough. And at the moment Aleko wanted her—that much was very clear. But it would not last. And she was not the type of person who could indulge in a physical relationship and come out of it unscathed. If she gave herself to a man she gave her all, her heart, her body, her soul.

She looked down at her hands clenched in her lap. 'The first time I saw you you reminded me of Greg. From a distance you have the same physical appearance. You bumped into a girl—at Heathrow—and you spent several minutes apparently apologising. I saw her face as you walked away, and you'd created quite an impression. I met Greg in exactly the same manner. He had the same practised charm as you, and I fell for it hook, line and sinker.'

'Let's get one thing quite clear, Kara,' Aleko said grimly. 'Whomever I marry she will never need to worry that I might lust after someone else. I admit that at the moment I date many girls, but the one I give my love to will have my devoted loyalty for the rest of her life.'

Her brows rose. 'Greg said that. Words are easy.'

He looked cross. 'I happen to mean it.'

She shrugged. 'It doesn't really interest me whether you do or not.'

'I think you're lying, Kara. I think you're more interested in me than you care to admit—even to yourself.'

'So,' she shrugged, 'you're physically attractive—I'll admit that. You're the first man who's made any impression on me since Greg died. But I'm not into affairs, if that's what you're after.'

'I'm offering my company,' he said. 'You could do with someone to restore your faith in human nature.'

'And you could do that?' she asked sceptically.

'If you'd let me.'

Kara shook her head. 'I don't believe it. You'd never settle for a platonic friendship—and I'd never settle for anything more. So what's the point?'

His mouth tightened. 'How did you find out about Greg's infidelity?'

'The hard way,' she snapped, wishing he hadn't started this pointless conversation. Today had been her happiest day in a long time, and now he was raking up the embers of her past—and spoiling everything.

'Go on,' he encouraged softly.

She let out a deep breath. 'It was everyone's nightmare come true. I was on my way home from work when I saw a car swerve to avoid a child, then veer out of control across the road and smash into a lamppost. Naturally I ran across to help. I can't tell you how I felt when I discovered the driver was Greg. He was dead.'

The moment came back to her with sickening clarity and she paused, feeling once again the full horror of the situation. When she began again her voice was much quieter. 'It was the same sort of car as Greg's, I'd realised that, but I never expected it to be him. He worked miles the other side of town.'

When Aleko would have spoken she silenced him with

a shake of her head. 'He wasn't alone. There was a woman with him, practically naked beneath her coat, and very much alive, screaming at my husband, shaking him, imploring him to wake up. I felt sick, so sick. I knew then that all the warnings I'd had about him were true. I staggered away, and when I finally got home the police were there.'

'And you've lived a life of hell ever since?' Aleko asked softly.

'Let's say it hasn't left me with much faith in human nature.' Kara closed her eyes and when the next moment she felt his arms about her she had no thought to resist.

'I think,' he said at length, 'that I'd better take you back to the Hythes. I didn't intend to put you through that. I never realised.'

'Not many people do,' she admitted, surprised by his compassion. She had expected a further emphatic denial that all men weren't the same.

He put her gently from him and set the jeep in motion, and Kara felt warmed towards him. Would it hurt to have an affair with Aleko after all? Would it not restore some of her self-confidence which had been badly crushed when she discovered Greg still needed other women? It had not been pleasant discovering she was not able to satisfy him, despite her belief that their sex life was good. Obviously she had not been good enough for him. A no-strings-attached affair might be the very antidote she needed.

But Aleko did not mention seeing her again. He gave her hand a comforting squeeze when he dropped her off, looked as though he was about to say something but changed his mind, then turned the jeep in an arc on the drive and roared back the way they had come.

Kara felt sad, and disappointed, but she could not

blame him. She had made it clear that she had no intention of indulging in an affair. He could not know that she had changed her mind.

The house was empty, but she heard the twins squealing in the pool, both now completely recovered from their illness. She would join them. A vigorous swim was what she needed to rid her system of unhappy thoughts.

Amanda and Damien were delighted, and Kara spent the next hour participating in their games and thoroughly wearing herself out.

After lunch the children went to bed as usual and Sharon asked Kara whether she would mind keeping an eye on them. 'If I don't get away from this place for an hour I shall go mad!' she said, with one of her persuasive smiles.

Kara could sympathise with her. During their illness Sharon hadn't had a moment to herself. In fact she looked quite peaky. 'Sneaking out to meet your boyfriend?' she joked, hoping her sister might at last confide.

'What boyfriend?' snapped Sharon. 'I wish you wouldn't keep prying!'

Kara lifted her hands. 'I'm sorry, I thought that—— Oh, Sharon, we used to be so close. What's happened? Why won't you talk to me any more?'

'I don't know what you mean,' said the younger girl huffily, a faint flush tinging her pale cheeks.

'You've changed. You're not the same. Who is this man that he must be kept secret? Are you afraid I won't approve? Is he married? Is that it?'

Sharon closed her eyes. 'I don't want to talk about him, Kara. Can't you accept that? I've not seen him recently. In fact I don't know whether I shall see him again.'

She looked close to tears, and Kara wisely said no more. The affair had obviously come to an end, in which case time alone would be Sharon's healer.

Another day passed and then to Kara's surprise and delight Aleko appeared before breakfast. 'I have business to attend to in Corfu,' he announced, looking directly at her. 'I'd like you to come with me.'

His dark eyes met hers and her heart fluttered like a caged bird. Without hesitation she said, 'I'd like that. Thank you.'

Rosemary and Geoff exchanged glances. They had no idea she had changed her mind about him. Aleko smiled, after first looking faintly surprised by her enthusiasm. Perhaps he had expected a fight on his hands? 'Good,' he said. 'As soon as you're ready we'll go.'

Sharon's eyes were also upon her. But why not indulge in a holiday romance? Fun while it lasted. Thank you and goodbye at the end.

Within fifteen minutes Kara was in his car and they were speeding towards the harbour. 'I'm glad you've agreed to come,' he said, sending her a smile that threatened to melt her bones in front of his very eyes.

'I decided I needed more stimulating company than the twins,' she replied lightly.

His eyes twinkled. 'That's interesting. I hope I don't disappoint you.'

Kara realised what she had said, and laughed. 'Don't get the wrong idea!' But she did not care even if he did. She was enjoying Aleko's company more and more. Yesterday had dragged. She had missed him dreadfully. He was good for her—both mentally and physically. She was beginning to feel all woman again.

Within five minutes they reached the tiny port. His boat was an impressive blue and white cabin cruiser, and Kara climbed on board, exploring eagerly as he started the engine. There were two cabins and a bathroom, the main living area and a galley. All immaculate, compact and—intimate was the word that sprang to mind. How many girls had he entertained here? she asked herself, and wondered why she felt hurt.

Once they had left Lakades she stood by him at the wheel, shading her eyes from the dazzling sun, smilingly accepting a peaked cap which made her feel like a sailor.

'How long will it take us to get to Corfu?' she asked.

'About an hour.'

'And what are your plans once we get there?'

He smiled. 'We'll do whatever you wish.'

She frowned. 'But I thought——'

'Exactly what I wanted you to think. Would you have come with me if I'd said I wanted to spend the whole day in your company? That it wasn't business that was taking me to Corfu, but an intense desire to see more of you?'

'Actually,' she said, seeing no reason why she should lie, 'I would still have come. I've decided you're good for me.'

His brows rose. 'Progress indeed! I think, Kara Lincroft, that you and I are on the same wavelength at last.' He hooked a hand round her waist and pulled her against him, and her body reacted immediately to his powerful sexuality.

'I'm not sure,' he said, flicking a playful finger against her cheek, 'whether I want to go to Corfu after all. After that little revelation I think I might keep you prisoner here and have my wanton way with you.' He looked at her questioningly. 'You look as though you wouldn't be averse to my suggestion?'

Kara closed her eyes and swallowed a choking lump in her throat. 'Actually, Aleko, I wouldn't. But I'm not going to let you.'

She heard his swift intake of breath, but his voice was serious when he spoke again. 'I wouldn't do that to you, Kara—you're not ready yet. But I'm glad you told me how you feel. It's pretty strong, isn't it, this emotion of ours?'

She nodded and looked into the hot blackness of his eyes, and felt herself drowning.

Aleko groaned and held her close, and Kara wondered if she were falling in love. Lord, she hoped not. What a disaster that would be! It was not in the plan of things at all.

But he was so considerate and kind and gentle and protective—as though he really cared. He held her cradled against him, one hand stroking her face, his other on the wheel. She could feel the unsteady throb of his heart and knew what it must be costing.

'You're so beautiful, Kara.' He tilted her face so that he could see every curve and every contour, every expression that came into her eyes, every breath she took. 'I want you so much.'

His hand moved from her face to the soft skin below her ears, sliding his fingers down her throat to her shoulders, feeling the quivers of pleasure that rippled through her, and he could contain himself no longer. He forgot the wheel and followed the course of his hands with his lips, and Kara thought she was going to faint with the sheer ecstasy of it all. Then he slid down the straps of her cotton suntop, pausing only fractionally to see whether she intended stopping him, baring her breasts to his hungry eyes—and his hands—and his mouth.

Kara's whole body throbbed and she made animal noises of hunger, straining her hips against him, feeling his arousal, digging her fingertips into his back as her heartbeats echoed in her head.

She could not believe it when he stopped, when he lifted his head, his lips soft and moist from tasting her, his eyes feasting for a few seconds more on her swollen breasts before replacing her suntop and pulling her into the curve of his arm.

'That will do—for now,' he said, in response to her faint cry of protest. 'It's sufficient that you trust me enough to—to want me to make love to you. You do want that?'

Shyly she nodded.

'We mustn't rush things,' he said. 'I'm very happy that you've changed your mind about me. In fact I'm almost scared in case I do or say the wrong thing.'

Aleko scared? Who was he trying to kid? A more confident man she had never met. 'I don't think there's any fear of that,' she whispered. 'I'm alive again, sexually alive, for the first time in ages—thanks to you.'

'And I intend making your arousal slow and sweet,' he muttered.

How could it be slow when her pulses were racing along and overtaking each other? When her blood scorched her skin, when every nerve-end was attuned to his lightest touch?

She wished she dared think that this meant more to Aleko than mere physical desire. Would he be so considerate if it were his bodily functions only that were involved? Surely not. It went deeper than that, for both of them. Maybe this wouldn't be a simple holiday romance after all.

Her thoughts ran on, and by the time they reached Corfu she felt as though she was floating on cloud nine. They left the boat hand in hand and wandered through the narrow flagstoned streets of Corfu old town. She felt carefree and young again and kept laughing into Aleko's eyes.

They took a ride in a canopied carriage drawn by a hatted horse, and he pulled her once again into his arms and kissed her. Kara felt herself spinning into space as his lips moved sensually over hers, and forgetting they were on full view to the public, she linked her hands behind his head, her lips parting to accept his probing tongue. They were locked in time by the flames of a mutual desire.

After the ride they had lunch in a crowded café overlooking the old Fortress, and Kara's awareness of Aleko increased by the second. He played with her fingers across the table, and her warmth had nothing at all to do with the heat of the sun. 'Have you been to Corfu before?' he asked softly.

Kara nodded. 'On my honeymoon,' she answered without thinking.

Aleko's lips tightened and suddenly he did not look quite so friendly. In fact his eyes were positively fierce and he let go her hands as though they were contaminated. 'So we're going over old ground? Why didn't you say? We could have gone somewhere else.'

'It doesn't matter,' she assured him, puzzled by his reaction. 'We stayed in Paleokastritsa. The only time we came here was to go to the casino.'

'He was a gambling man?' growled Aleko, his fingers clenching.

Kara felt hurt by his sudden anger. 'Actually, no,' she said strongly. 'It was not one of his bad habits.'

He glared at her suspiciously. 'You sound almost as though you're defending him?'

'And why shouldn't I?' she demanded, his anger transferring itself to her. 'He was my husband.'

'Your unfaithful husband,' he sneered, glowering from beneath his thick brows, making it impossible for her to imagine that only minutes earlier he had made her feel cherished and desired.

'Heavens!' she exploded, her eyes flashing a brilliant blue. 'I'm beginning to wish I hadn't told you about him!' He really was going too far. 'I'm willing to be friends with you, Aleko, but I don't want to discuss Greg.'

'Nor do I,' he thrust heavily, 'although I have the strangest feeling that he's going to intrude whether we like it or not.' He scraped his chair loudly back from the table. 'Let's get away from here—I've had enough!'

Kara failed to understand why he should get so worked up about her late husband. In just over a week she would be gone and he wouldn't see her again. He was offering her an affair, that was all, nothing serious. What did it matter whether she had been here with Greg or not?

To her surprise he hailed a taxi and when they were seated he said, 'I have some relatives in the mountains. It's time I paid them a visit.'

Kara hardly thought visiting some of Aleko's family was the right thing to do under the circumstances. If he'd had enough of her shouldn't they go back to Lakades? It was amazing how quickly her euphoria had disappeared.

He sat scowling while she looked out of the window.

The scenery was breathtaking, she had to admit. Cypress trees speared the rolling hills, standing tall above the lush green of the other vegetation, adding a whole new dimension to the landscape. And far below was the backdrop of blue, blue sea. It was an exchanting island, and it was a pity Aleko had developed this black mood.

The road crept upwards, snaking round hairpin bends, becoming less and less smooth, until finally they were bumping over potholes that were a threat to the car's suspension, and all that was between their wheels and a drop of several hundred feet was a few inches of loose rubble.

Kara closed her eyes, losing all interest in the scenery, and clinging to the edge of her seat until her fingers ached. Aleko seemed not to notice that she was scared. What had happened to the consideration he had shown earlier?

They came upon the villa unexpectedly, impressive with its terraced garden and swimming pool, and jutting balconies skirted with wrought iron.

He paid the driver and as they climbed the steps to the iron gates a girl in her early twenties came racing out. She was slim and graceful, her shining black hair drawn tightly back from a face that was strikingly beautiful. All she wore was a yellow bikini.

There was radiance in her eyes as she flung herself at Aleko, rattling off a question in Greek. Without giving him the opportunity to answer she planted her lips full on his, and his arms went around her and he swung her off her feet.

Kara watched, feeling choked inside, even though she knew it was wrong. Whoever this girl was it had nothing to do with her. Had Aleko known she would be here?

Was that why he had suggested this visit? She, Kara, had disappointed him and he wished to seek relief elsewhere.

When he put the girl back down he was smiling, and his eyes had lost their hardness. He glanced at Kara almost as if he had forgotten she was there. 'Ah, Kara, meet Katina. Katina, this is Kara Lincroft. She is holidaying with the Hythes. You remember Rosemary and Geoff?'

The girl nodded but gave Kara no more than a brief smile before looking back up at Aleko. Her head reached his shoulder. She looked dainty and fragile against the toughness of him and they walked towards the house, their arms linked about each other's waists, leaving Kara to bring up the rear.

She wanted to turn and leave, but he had dismissed the taxi and it was a long way to go, so she seethed and followed, wishing she had never agreed to come out with him.

Sitting indoors was a man who looked in his fifties, though he could have been younger. His hair was grey and his face lined and gaunt. He looked ill, or as though he had been ill, and he didn't get up when they entered the room.

Aleko went across to him and took his extended hand in both of his, speaking in their native language, and then finally turning to introduce Kara. 'Kara is out here from England for a holdiay. Kara, my cousin Thimios.'

Kara shook his hand and smiled hesitantly. His grip was surprisingly firm and his eyes were warm and welcoming. 'England is my favourite place, next to Greece, of course.' His English was more heavily accented than Aleko's. 'Forgive me for not getting up.'

'Thimios had an accident,' cut in Aleko, instantly

aware of the other man's distress. 'He doesn't get out much these days, so he'll be glad of someone new to talk to. I think I might take a dip in the pool with Katina. You don't mind?'

Kara did mind, she would have liked a swim too, but he was already half out of the room. She swallowed her disappointment and turned back to Thimios, who was watching her face closely.

'Go after them,' he said kindly. 'You do not have to stay with me.'

She gave a tiny shake of her head. 'Two's company, three's a crowd.'

'Then come and sit down. You must forgive my daughter, she thinks the world of Aleko. My wife and I lived on Lakades for the first few years of our married life and Katina idolised him. Though with a twelve-year age gap he did not have much time for her, as you can imagine.'

'I see,' said Kara.

'When my uncle, that is Aleko's father, remarried— his first wife died when Aleko was eleven—although I expect you know all this?—Aleko acquired a new half-brother who was nearer Katina's own age, and she transferred her allegiance. She and Petros are very close, and any day now I am expecting to hear they want to get married, but she still has a great affection for Aleko, and he for her, and she loves it when he comes to visit us.'

'Thank you for telling me, but you didn't have to,' said Kara softly, wondering if he were so frank with everyone he met. 'Aleko and I aren't—we're not—we're just—acquaintances. My sister is nanny to the Hythes' children and I've come over for a holiday. Aleko's very kind, but there's nothing at all between us.' She did not realise how sad she sounded.

'But you wish there was?' Thimios looked at her knowingly. 'Actually you are the first girl Aleko has brought here, so you must forgive me for thinking you were someone special. How much holiday have you left?'

'Another week,' admitted Kara.

'Plenty of time,' he said, more to himself than to her.

For what? she wondered. To indulge in an affair? To fall in love? No chance of that, not now. If he was going to be funny every time Greg was mentioned there would be no point in it.

And then he noticed her wedding ring. 'You are married?'

'I'm a widow,' she confessed quietly. 'My husband died in a road accident two years ago.' With his latest girlfriend at his side, she added silently and bitterly. The thought still had the power to hurt.

'I am sorry. I too was in such an accident. I was lucky, though. It is difficult for me to walk, but at least I am still alive.'

And he called that luck? She wondered where his wife was? She was almost afraid to ask in case she too had been involved.

As if reading her thoughts he said, 'I am sorry my wife is not here. She would love to meet you, I know. She has gone to visit her sister in Rome, at my insistence. She rarely moves from my side these days, and I feel so guilty.'

'You shouldn't,' said Kara at once. 'I imagine it's a labour of love so far as she's concerned.' Outside she could hear his daughter laughing and Aleko's deep guffaw, and wished their budding relationship had not been ruined. Her last week here could have been so enjoyable.

She guessed Greg would always come between them. Whether he was mentioned or not he was there, an invisible barrier. It was her own fault. These last two years she had done nothing to forget him—a form of masochism, she supposed.

'You are looking sad,' said Thimios.

Kara's mouth twisted wryly. 'I was miles away, I'm sorry.'

'You were thinking of your husband?'

She nodded, though if he had read her mind he would know it was not sorrow that had tempered her thoughts.

'It does not do to dwell too much on the past. You have to make a new life for yourself. It is a matter of adapting.'

He was right, of course, but there was more to it than that. The promise of a few days laughing and loving had been snatched from beneath her very eyes. Not only by Greg, but by this man's daughter. Katina was the balm Aleko needed following his disappointment over her.

They chatted some more and then Katina and Aleko returned, dripping and laughing and looking as though they'd had a whale of a time.

'Katina's invited us to dinner,' said Aleko. 'It will mean us staying overnight. I'll phone through to the Hythes so they won't worry. You've no objections?'

CHAPTER FOUR

ALEKO apparently had a change of clothes at Thimios's house, left there from a previous visit, but Kara was compelled to borrow from Katina.

They had spent the afternoon sipping tea and inevitably discussing the wine trade, and now it was time to get ready for dinner. Kara had grown steadily jealous of the rapport that existed between Katina and Aleko, and as she followed the girl up to her room she wondered how she was going to get through the evening.

'How about this one?' asked Katina airily, pulling a cerise-coloured dress out of her wardrobe. 'I never wear it because it's too big. It should fit you perfectly.'

Ouch! thought Kara, feeling gross. Had the girl no tact? There couldn't be more than one size between them.

'I cannot tell you how pleased I am that Aleko came here today,' Katina went on. 'How long have you known him?'

'A week, that's all,' shrugged Kara.

'It's the first time he's brought a girl here.'

'So your father told me. I hope I'm not intruding. He kind of sprung it on me and I had no choice.'

'That's Aleko,' announced the dark girl. 'He's so masterful!' She sounded as though she admired him for it. 'The girl he marries will have to be strong, there is no doubt about that. You are already married, I see?'

'I'm a widow,' said Kara, hoping she didn't have to go through the explanations all over again.

Katina's dark brows rose. 'And so you are looking for a new man? What are your feelings for Aleko?'

Kara was unaccustomed to such bluntness and resented the girl's probing, especially as she was still vulnerable from Aleko's earlier lovemaking. 'I don't see that it's any of your business. Why do you ask?'

'Most girls Aleko takes out fall madly in love with him. I wanted to warn you that he is not the marrying kind.'

'I know that,' replied Kara with quiet dignity. 'I'm not yet ready to marry again, but if I were it certainly wouldn't be to someone like Aleko.' Not a man whose mood changed like the wind.

Katina looked sceptical, as if wondering how any woman could possible resist him. 'So what sort of man are you looking for?'

'If I were looking for a man he would be one I could trust,' she said simply. 'One who would look after me and never hurt me.'

'And you think Aleko has not those qualifications?'

Kara looked at the other girl coolly. 'I don't know him well enough to say whether he has or not.' There were times when she thought he had, others when she was not so sure. He could be the kindest man on the face of the earth, he could also be the most hateful.

Katina abruptly changed the subject. 'Have you met Petros?'

'No, I haven't,' admitted Kara slowly. 'Your father told me that you and he are——'

'I love Petros,' said the girl with a smile. 'I do not see him as often as I would like—Aleko makes him work hard. But it is good that he should learn the business. One day he and Aleko will run it together.'

She sounded proud of her young man, and they

continued to talk as they showered and changed and Kara discovered that Katina was really quite likeable.

The girl's feelings towards Aleko were more those of a protective sister than anything else, which Kara found amusing, considering Aleko was well capable of looking after himself. Given the chance it looked as though Katina would personally vet any girl he took an interest in.

Kara wondered whether he had ever loved a girl enough to want to marry her? It seemed odd that he should be in his thirties and still single. No sooner did the thought occur to her than she put it to Katina.

'There was a girl once,' admitted the Greek girl reluctantly. 'I was really sure they would get married. Aleko thought the world of her.'

'So what happened?' asked Kara.

Katina lifted her slender shoulders. 'No one knows. She suddenly disappeared out of his life and he refused to discuss her. If I dare to ask him he snaps my head off.'

Maybe he'd had a taste of what he'd done to others, thought Kara, sleeking her hair into place and taking a last look at herself through the mirror. If so he deserved it, and she could feel no pity. Men thought women were toys to be played with and discarded when they had finished with them. Was this dress really suitable? Katina could wear these vibrant colours, but they drained Kara's already pale skin and she really preferred something more muted.

'Are you ready?' asked Katina, looking radiant in a peacock blue strapless dress that clung seductively to her curves. She wore no jewellery and her high-heeled sandals echoed the colour of her dress. She looked irresistible, and Kara wondered how Aleko could possibly not be interested.

In contrast she felt that the bright pinky-red she had been forced to wear made her look common, it was low-cut and short, and the fact that Katina's feet were a size smaller than her own meant she had to wear the flat sandals she had worn all day. They had looked good with shorts but were unsuitable with this dress. She felt ugly and wished there was some way she could get out of this dinner. Maybe she could feign a headache? But already Katina had opened the door and was waiting for her to follow.

The fact that Aleko looked devastating and immaculate in a sky blue shirt and grey slacks made Kara angrier still. And it did not help that his eyes slid insolently over the unfortunate dress, resting a fraction too long on her cleavage before studying the length of her legs, his lips curving when he saw the unbecoming sandals.

She smiled a greeting at Thimios but scowled at his cousin and pretended an interest in the view from the window.

The sun was going down behind the mountain and the slopes below were dark and mysterious. Its huge shadow reached almost to the shoreline where the sea still glittered and danced. A white liner threaded its way slowly across the horizon, and beyond was the hazy purple coastline of Albania.

A hand on her shoulder made her jump and she turned. Aleko towered above her, his brows drawn together. 'Is something wrong?'

'Why should there be?' she demanded, her tone sickly sweet.

'There's no reason at all,' he returned slowly and deliberately, 'except that your look just now told me otherwise. Don't you like Katina? Didn't you get on with her? Would you rather we didn't stay here tonight?'

'Katina has nothing at all to do with the way I'm feeling at this particular moment,' Kara flung crossly. 'It's just that—well, if you must know, it's because you look so damned smart and I feel like a freak.'

His mouth quivered as he tried to suppress a grin. 'A very beautiful freak. The dress isn't your usual style, I agree, but it's delightfully revealing. I have no complaints.'

'It's the only one Katina said would fit me,' Kara hissed through her teeth. 'She more or less accused me of being fat!'

This time Aleko laughed out loud. 'Katina's too thin, you don't want to be like her. I prefer my women shapely.' Again his eyes dropped to her breasts and Kara felt an impossible heat invade her skin. Oh, lord, was she so weak that one look, one kind word, would have her melting in his arms all over again?

He touched the back of his fingers to her cheek, letting them trail slowly and sensually down her throat and over her curves exposed by the too-low dress. 'You look good to me, Kara,' he muttered, 'and Uncle Thimios thinks you're some woman too. He's done nothing but sing your praises.'

Kara looked beyond him to where the older man sat in his chair. Katina was by his side chatting happily, but he glanced across and caught her eye, and his warm smile, coupled with Aleko's praise, made Kara feel infinitely better.

'It was wrong of me to try and make you jealous with Katina. I was still angry about Greg. What a swine he was! You deserve better than that. Am I forgiven?' His dark eyes rested intently on her face.

She nodded. How could she not forgive Aleko when he was in this mood?

Later, in bed, Kara reflected that dinner hadn't been the ordeal she expected. On the contrary, she had been made most welcome, both Aleko and Thimios taking great pains to include her in the conversation. Aleko sat at her side, Thimios opposite with Katina, and it was no accident that Aleko's thigh occasionally brushed hers.

Excitement had mounted in her veins and now her body ached with needing him. He was in the next room and she could hear him moving about. She wondered what he would say if she knocked on his door and asked whether she might spend the night with him. She giggled to herself, though she had a feeling he wouldn't be shocked. In fact he was probably thinking about her too.

The more she thought about it, the less inclined she was to sleep, and after a couple of hours spent tossing and turning she decided a cup of hot milk might be the answer. She was sure Thimios wouldn't mind her helping herself.

She groped her way along the landing and down the stairs, thankful for the moonlight slanting its way through the windows. She did not want to put on the light and maybe disturb the other occupants of the house.

Once in the kitchen she closed the door and only then did she snap on the light, blinking as its brightness hurt her eyes. She found milk in the fridge and filled a mug, popping it into the microwave. Then she sat quietly and sipped it, feeling the liquid soothe and relax, and when she tiptoed back up the stairs some minutes later she felt better.

She pushed open the bedroom door and stepped

inside, closed it gently and tiptoed across the room. She had left her curtains drawn so there was no moonlight to guide her, but it was only a few strides to the bed.

Holding back the sheet, she slid inside—and then cried out in alarm as her leg touched another body! Aleko? He had crept in while she was downstairs.

He seemed to be asleep. At least he hadn't spoken, or moved, and she touched him experimentally again, her heart thumping. He was naked!

She was about to withdraw when his hand shot out and grasped her arm. 'Oh, no, you don't!'

'Let go of me!' she muttered angrily. 'What the hell do you think you're playing at? Talk about not wanting to rush things! My God, you have a nerve!' She forgot that only minutes earlier she had contemplated creeping into his room. He snapped on the bedside lamp and it cast shadows over the angles of his face. He looked amused. 'You're asking me what I'm doing? Don't you think it should be the other way round?'

'Why?' she demanded, conscious of the light filtering through the skimpy nylon nightdress Katina had lent her. It hid nothing. She might as well have been naked herself. 'You jump into my bed while I'm out, why should you be the one to ask questions?'

'Your bed?' His amusement deepened.

'Yes, my bed,' she snapped.

Holding back the laughter that was bubbling inside him, he said, 'I think you ought to take a good look around.'

Frowning, Kara glanced about her—and saw his clothes on the chair, his shoes on the floor. Oh lord, she was in the wrong room!

'I'm sorry,' she said at once. 'I went down for a drink. I made a mistake. What must you be thinking?'

'That it's a pity you want to go.' Aleko pulled her closer towards him. 'I was dreaming about you, Kara.'

She looked into the dark depths of his eyes—and then wished she hadn't when she was caught and held by an inner power. Sudden sensation ran through her and her body responded to his as completely as it had on the boat.

This was what she had wanted, what she had desperately needed, yet now an opportunity had presented itself she felt afraid. It would be so easy to become too involved. Aleko was a dangerously attractive man, and she wanted no bonds to hold her.

'If you let me go you can carry on dreaming,' she said lightly, tugging again, but to no avail.

He sat up and the sheet slid off him, revealing his deeply tanned chest with its scattering of dark hairs. Kara had a ridiculous urge to run her fingers through them. He slid his free arm behind her back and urged her towards him.

Kara closed her eyes, took a deep breath, and gave up. Her whole body was attuned to him, crying out in response to his total masculinity. It had been a long time, a long, long time. When his mouth closed on hers her lips parted and their tongues entwined and she pressed herself urgently against him.

He drank deeply of her mouth, his kiss drugging her, seducing her, and she let him slip her nightie over her head without a murmur. The feel of his hair-roughened skin against her naked breasts incited her to even greater awareness, and she moaned softly and unconsciously, and moved erotically against him.

He slid down the bed and she followed. His hands explored each curve and each hollow of her body, inciting and exciting, torturing, teasing. Kara moaned and writhed with the sweet agony of it all and moved even closer to his hard demanding body.

Sex with Greg had never been like this. Her whole
being felt as though it was engulfed in flames, desire
curled her stomach into tight knots, and she wanted to
be a part of Aleko, wanted to melt into him, feel him,
taste him.

He framed her face with his hands and looked deep
into her eyes, his voice low and sexy as he murmured
something in Greek. Whatever he said it sounded good,
and she ran the tip of her tongue over her lips, her mouth
dry, her body crying out for fulfilment.

His mouth met hers and he renewed his assault of her
senses, his hand moulding itself to the contours of her
breast, a firm leg thrust between her thighs. Her whole
body pulsed with desire and she arched herself towards
him, all sane reasoning dispelled.

'Aleko,' she husked, not even conscious of what she
was saying. 'Oh, Aleko, how I want you!'

'And me you,' he muttered. 'I've wanted you from
the moment I first saw you. Kara, *agape mou*, you've
been driving me insane, do you know that? I promised
myself I would take things slowly, but I can't wait any
longer. You feel good, so good!'

With an even deeper hunger his mouth drank of hers,
moving over her face and her breasts, and all a woman's
secret places, until Kara was almost driven out of her
mind and was past the point of no return.

When their bodies finally fused she felt mindless, as
though she had been blown into a million pieces. It was
like scaling the highest mountain and soaring from its
peak to the heavens. Never, ever, even in the early days
with Greg, had she reached such a climax of sensation.

They lay quietly locked in each other's arms, their
skin moist, their heartbeats thundering. Part of her had

been lost to Aleko. She had freely given and he had taken, and nothing would ever be the same again.

She had promised herself this would be a fun affair, but she had not expected this depth of feeling. It bound her to him. She wondered whether he felt the same, or whether it meant nothing. Men had a stronger sex urge than women and never let their emotions get involved. With them it was purely physical—which was what she had intended—but now she was not so sure. Her feelings ran deeper than that.

Her husband was the only other man who had made love to her, and she had always felt very strongly about sex outside marriage. Only the fact that she had suffered two depressing years had made her cast her inhibitions to the wind now—and she had fully expected that she could get up and walk away. What a foolish thought it had been!

Cradled in Aleko's arms and fully sated by his lovemaking, Kara slept. When she woke the following morning she felt an unaccustomed excitement lingering in her veins, but it took her a moment or two to realise where she was and what was the cause of it.

Smiling dreamily, she turned her head, but the bed beside her was empty. She thrust back the sheets and stood up, stretching her arms above her head, feeling a glorious sense of well-being.

Aleko chose that moment to enter the room, his eyes resting instantly and hungrily on her naked body. He wore a towel about his loins, but nothing else, and his hair was crisp and damp and there was a clean fresh smell about him.

Kara felt no shyness, and when he dropped his towel she walked eagerly into his arms and they made love all over again.

'Aleko, that's enough!' she protested, when his hunger appeared insatiable. 'How do you expect me to appear normal before your cousin and Katina? Do you want them to know what we've been doing?'

He laughed. 'I want to tell the whole world. You're fantastic, Kara.'

'You too,' she responded fervently. 'I feel more alive than I have in a long time.'

'And this is only the beginning,' he taunted with a smile.

Of what? A week of making love whenever they could, and then an abrupt end to it all? Or the beginning of a much deeper and longer relationship? Such were her feelings at this moment that if he had suggested she live with him on his island home she would willingly have agreed.

But she did not voice her thoughts. They were happy ones and she did not wish to dampen them with disillusionment.

'I think I ought to take a shower,' she said softly.

'Would you like me to join you?'

She dimpled prettily. 'Yes, but you'd better not.'

'You're right,' he said, cupping her face and running the tip of his tongue sensually over her lips before kissing her. 'We might dissolve in the steam and never be seen again. Get going.' He gave her bottom a smart pat and she ran for the door.

'Don't forget this.'

Kara turned and caught her nightie, hugging it to her chest as she slid into the next room. Her heart was banging fit to burst and she felt deliriously happy and glad to be alive.

Breakfast was a lighthearted meal. Thimios's knowing eye was on them both, but Katina was fortunately out.

Her mother was returning that day and she had driven to the airport to meet her.

Kara hated to think what the girl would have to say if she saw the impression Aleko had made on her. She felt warm and glowing and knew it was visible, and she was glad when Aleko apologised and said they couldn't stay to meet Phrosini. 'Give her my love,' he said, 'and tell her I'll be back soon.'

'Both of you, I hope?' said Thimios.

'Maybe,' grinned Aleko.

I trust so, added Kara silently.

During the drive down the mountain Kara seemed to have a permanently silly smile fixed to her face, and whenever Aleko glanced across at her she felt her insides begin to melt.

'Happy?' he asked.

She nodded. Deliriously, she would have liked to say, but was afraid to tempt fate. It couldn't last. This was a holiday affair, and she must remember that at all costs.

'Thank you for coming to me last night.'

'I'm glad I did,' she whispered. What a happy mistake it had been! Their bodies were so completely attuned that it was as though they were made for each other. Common sense told her this could never be, but it would not hurt to dream for a while.

'If I didn't have an important meeting to attend I would spend the whole day on my boat making love to you,' warned Aleko, his hand resting possessively on her thigh, triggering of a whole new flurry of excitement inside her.

Kara glanced at him provocatively from beneath her silky lashes. 'You're greedy!'

'The idea doesn't appeal?' His brows raised in mock disbelief.

She closed her eyes and resting her head back on the seat took a deep much-needed breath. 'Very much so.'

He groaned. 'Oh, Kara, what you do to me!'

And he to her. 'I will see you again, before I return to England?' she asked huskily.

'What do you think?'

She looked into the dark depths of his eyes. 'I think you might arrange it.'

'I think I might,' he smiled.

They wound down the hill and he had to concentrate on the road, but whereas on the way up Kara had spent her time looking at the scenery, this time it was on Aleko her eyes rested.

And just looking at him set her heart in top gear, her pulses racing to keep up. His deeply tanned face was strong and purposeful, with a ruggedness which added to his attraction. His hands on the wheel were long and masculine, and it was difficult to realise how gently and sensually they had stroked her body.

There was no need for words. They had built up a surprising rapport and there was comfort in sitting silently beside him. Occasionally he would glance across and smile, a smile that held warmth and hunger, a smile full of promises. Her stomach churned and her cheeks burnt, and she marvelled at their intimacy.

His boat sat serenely in the harbour, bobbing gently at her moorings, and Kara took Aleko's hand as he helped her on board. His grip tightened and he pulled her purposefully to him, kissing her full on the lips before allowing her to step down on to the deck.

He started the engine and cast off, and soon they had left Corfu behind. She stood beside him at the wheel, his arm about her shoulders, and she didn't want the short crossing to end.

'Your husband was a fool,' he muttered once, but Kara pretended she had not heard. She had no wish to enter into another heated discussion about Greg.

Halfway to Lakades, when no land at all was in sight, he cut the engines and let the boat drift. There was no wind, the sea was oil-smooth, and he knew they would not go far off course.

He took her below deck and into his cabin, where they made love on his bed, and Kara had never felt so happy in her life.

Afterwards, tucked into the circle of his arm, she posed a question that had been constantly on her mind during the last few hours. 'Why haven't you ever married, Aleko?'

He was silent for so long she thought he was not going to answer, then he said quietly, 'There are reasons.'

'Katina told me there was a girl once whom you cared very much about. What happened to her?'

He stiffened abruptly. 'Katina had no right discussing my private life!'

'She was trying to warn me off you.'

A smile flickered, 'She's very protective.'

Kara nodded. 'I had noticed. I think she's half in love with you herself.'

'Katina?' he frowned. 'She's just a child.'

'Probably the same age as me. Do you think I'm a child?'

Aleko's eyes softened. 'You're all woman, Kara, make no mistake about that!'

'So who was this girl?' she probed, feeling an irrational need to know more about this person who had once stolen his heart.

Abruptly he let go of her and stood up, pulling on his shorts, his face hard and stern. Kara felt a quiver of misgiving. 'I'm sorry, I ought not to have asked. It has nothing to do with me.'

'I want to tell you,' he said. 'But I haven't spoken to anyone about Cleo since—since it happened.' He grimaced ruefully. 'I'm very good at telling you to get things out of your system! Maybe I should do the same.'

Kara waited.

'We were going to get married. I loved her very much—and she loved me. Unfortunately she was promised to someone else.' Aleko paused, his mind going over the painful memories. 'She comes of a very old Greek family where they maintain all the traditions. Her father suffered a heart attack when he discovered our plans. On his deathbed he begged her to marry Dimitrios, and because—because she wanted to make him happy in his last hours, Cleo obeyed.'

His voice was gruff with emotion, and Kara's heart went out to him. 'I can't believe it,' she exclaimed. 'How could she possibly marry a person she didn't love? I wouldn't do it, not even to please my parents.'

'The Greeks are a different race from the English. Family ties are very strong. In the end she could not go against them.'

'And—is she happy—with Dimitrios?'

He shrugged. 'I think so. I haven't seen her since—we decided it was best. Get dressed, Kara, we'd better be on our way.'

It was a sad story, she reflected, as she pulled on her shorts and top. She would have liked to ask how long ago it had happened but was afraid to risk bringing up the subject again. She was flattered Aleko had told her so much.

As they stood together at the rail it was not long before his arm snaked round her and his kiss was long and hard, full of need. 'You're the first woman since Cleo who's really got through to me, do you know that?' Aleko asked huskily. 'And there have been plenty. But none who could do more than satisfy my manly needs.'

A thrill rode through her. Was this an admission of love? 'You're the first since Greg, too,' she admitted shyly.

'And I've been the recipient of all that bottled-up emotion?' He looked pleased by the thought. 'Perhaps the man did me a good turn after all.'

They teased and flirted until Lakades was reached, and then he whisked her back to the Hythes' villa in his car and reluctantly said goodbye. 'I shall only just make that meeting,' he remarked, glancing at his watch.

'Dressed like that?' she taunted.

'Minx! I have to go home and change first. May I see you tonight?'

Such formality! She grinned. 'I think I might have to consult my diary.'

'I'll collect you at eight. We'll eat out and then I might take you to meet my parents.'

Kara's brows rose and her heart skipped a beat. 'I'm flattered, but why?'

'Because they're curious.'

'You've already told them about me?'

He nodded.

'What did you say?'

'That I'd met a very prim and proper English miss who wouldn't even let me kiss her. That you intrigued me and that I intended taking you to bed if it was the last thing I did.'

'Liar!' she laughed.

'You're beautiful,' Aleko said softly.

'And you're pretty gorgeous yourself.'

'I'll see you later.'

She nodded. 'I'll be ready.'

'You'd better be. I beat any girl who keeps me waiting.'

He revved up the engine, and Kara watched until he was out of sight. Then she walked into the house feeling on top of the world.

She went straight to her room and showered, glad to get out of the shorts and top she had worn for nearly two days. She pulled on a white, full-skirted sundress and looked at herself in the mirror. The sun had made her nose red and her face pink—she ought really to have taken more care. But there was a glow about her that had not been there before. Her eyes were shining, her lips permanently curved upwards. She looked—like a woman in love!

Was she? Or was it purely the excitement of a body chemistry that had taken over? She wanted to talk to someone about it, to share the exhilaration that she felt.

Through her window she saw the twins in the garden playing ball, Sharon lying on the grass watching. How surprised her sister would be when she heard what had happened!

She ran outside and threw herself down beside Sharon, smilingly shaking her head when Amanda and Damien clamoured for her to join them.

'Oh, Sharon, I've had a lovely time,' she began. 'Aleko and I are getting on like a house on fire. Did you miss me last night? We stayed at his cousin's. He's got a beautiful house.'

'Really,' said Sharon indifferently, lying back with her eyes closed.

'Yes, really. Don't you want to hear? I had to borrow some clothes from Katina, that's Aleko's first cousin

once removed. Gosh, what a sight I looked! But Aleko
didn't seem to mind. In fact he told me I looked
beautiful.' Kara pretended to preen herself, but it was
wasted when Sharon did not notice.

'What's the matter, Sharon?' She peered more closely
at her sister. 'You look pale. Aren't you well?'

'I'm all right,' said Sharon, sitting up and clasping
her hands round her knees. 'Hey, Damien, stop hitting
Amanda!'

'You look worried. What's happened? Is it that boy
again?' Why hadn't she noticed that something was
wrong with her sister instead of going off on that long
spiel about herself and Aleko? Sharon looked as though
she had all the cares of the world on her shoulders.

Tears suddenly filled Sharon's eyes and she dropped
her head down so that her long silky hair hid her face.
'Oh, Kara, what am I going to do? I think I'm
pregnant.'

CHAPTER FIVE

KARA'S heart stopped and she looked wide-eyed at her sister. 'Pregnant? How?' It was a stupid question, she knew that the moment she uttered it. 'I mean, I thought that—oh hell, Sharon, what have you been doing?'

Sharon's bowed shoulders shook, but she remained silent.

'Are you sure? Have you seen a doctor?'

Her sister shook her head. 'But I know. I'm long overdue, and I don't feel well. How am I going to tell the Hythes?'

'I think that's the least of your worries,' snapped Kara. 'For heaven's sake, Sharon, why did you get so deeply involved? Who is he? Have you told him?'

She thought about her own highly charged lovemaking with Aleko and thanked her lucky stars that for health reasons she had continued to take the pill since Greg's death.

'It's Petros,' admitted Sharon quietly. 'I told him last night. He's not very happy.'

Kara gasped. 'Petros? Aleko's half-brother?' The man Katina was going to marry!

Sharon nodded.

What a rotter! No wonder he was dismayed! This was something he clearly hadn't bargained for. And what an idiot her sister was. Why hadn't she taken care?

'Oh, Sharon!' She daren't tell her sister about Katina, not at this stage; the girl was unhappy enough. 'You'll have to speak to him again,' she said determinedly. 'The baby's as much his responsibility as yours.'

She felt appalled by the situation, shocked through and through. And it proved that no man was to be trusted, that they treated women as mere playthings and wanted none of the responsibilities of a home and family.

Thank goodness she had gone into her affair with Aleko with her eyes wide open. She would make sure that it remained nothing more than physical attraction, that she could walk away at the end of her holiday with her heart whole and her pride intact.

'I'm seeing him tonight,' admitted Sharon faintly.

'Do you love him?'

Her sister nodded, her teeth clenched, her lips pale.

'Has he ever mentioned marriage?' It was a question Kara had to ask even though she knew what the answer would be.

Miserably Sharon shook her head.

'Don't you think you ought to discuss it?'

'I don't want him to feel he's being trapped into something he's not ready for.'

'He might surprise you and suggest it himself, now he's had time to get used to the idea.' Kara wished she were as convinced as she tried to make herself sound.

'You think so?' Sharon's face brightened slightly. 'You really think so?'

'He's not much of a man if he doesn't,' Kara said sharply. 'The baby's as much his as yours.'

Amanda and Damien chose that moment to come racing up. 'Sharon, Sharon!' They tugged at her hands. 'We want to swim, we want to swim. Please, Sharon!'

Sharon let them pull her to her feet. She seemed relieved to put an end to the conversation. 'Come on then, I'll race you back to the house. Last one to get changed is a cissy!'

Kara was glad her sister wasn't taking it out on the twins. Perhaps they were the antidote she needed? Their boundless energy and incessant high spirits did not leave her much time to sit and brood.

She followed more sedately, deciding to join them, and the next hour passed so quickly that it was time for lunch before they knew it. Afterwards Sharon put the twins to bed and declared that she was going to lie down herself, which meant, Kara realised, that she did not want to discuss the matter further.

Sharon's revelation overshadowed her excitement about dining at Aleko's home tonight. It was so unlike her sister to be short-tempered and secretive that she ought to have guessed something serious was wrong. It should have been obvious.

She hoped and prayed that when Sharon spoke to Petros he would be more sympathetic. Obviously it had come as a great shock to him, but now surely he would consider Sharon before himself?

Later that afternoon Aleko phoned. Kara's heart quickened when she heard the throaty sound of his voice. 'Hello, Aleko,' she said, wondering why he was calling.

'I'm missing you,' he groaned. 'I've had a hell of a meeting. I've been unable to keep my mind on it for thinking about you.'

'I've missed you too,' she confessed huskily, closing her eyes and leaning back against the wall. His words had brought a new ache to her loins and she could almost feel him against her, his breath warm on her cheek, the scent of him filling her nostrils.

'I'm afraid I have some bad news,' he said.

She froze. Sharon? Petros had told him?

'I can't make it tonight.'

Kara breathed again.

'I have to host my American visitors. Their flight's been delayed twenty-four hours, and I had no alternative but to ask them to stay here.'

Disappointment welled in Kara's throat. The rest of her time here was so short that each day was becoming increasingly precious. She had been looking forward to tonight, even though meeting his parents might prove an ordeal.

'You can't help it,' she said in a quiet little voice.

'You're upset?'

She swallowed hard. 'Disappointed.'

'Me too. If there was any way out I'd take it, you must know that. I haven't felt so excited about a woman since——'

'Cleo?' she suggested softly.

'No, not Cleo. She was—different.'

He meant he had loved Cleo. Herself he simply desired. He saw her as a sex object only. Which she knew and accepted, of course. It was what she wanted—wasn't it?

'But you're special too, Kara, in your own delightful way,' Aleko continued. 'I'll be thinking of you—especially when I'm alone in my bed tonight.' His voice dropped to a meaningful growl.

'And me you,' she husked.

'Till tomorrow, then.'

'Tomorrow.'

'The same time?'

'Yes.'

Their voices grew fainter.

'I look forward to it.'

'Me as well.'

'*Cherete*, Kara.'

'Goodbye.'

The line went dead, and the hours until she saw him again promised to drag. Nor did she see Sharon until the following morning. She had lain awake listening for her sister to return from her rendezvous with Petros, but her own eventful night with Aleko had taken its toll, and she fell asleep before Sharon came in. She even overslept the next morning, waking to the sound of the twins' shrill cries as they splashed in the pool.

She showered and pulled on shorts and a simple top over her bikini, and after a hurried breakfast of toast and orange juice went outside to join them.

It was another blue halcyon day, and Kara decided she could get quite used to this life. Sharon sat on the edge of the pool, her feet dangling in the water, her watchful eyes on the children.

'Well,' said Kara, sitting beside her and dabbling her feet likewise, 'how did it go? What did Petros say?'

Sharon turned her face, and the instant Kara saw her eyes she knew. They were sad and haunted and miserable and she looked close to tears. 'He won't marry me. He won't tell me the reason, he just says he can't.'

Kara knew, and anger welled up inside her. What a two-timing devil he was! He had not even the courage to tell Sharon about Katina. 'It means, of course, he doesn't love you, he's been playing around, the same as all men,' she said sharply. 'I'm surprised at you, Sharon. You should have known and made sure nothing like this happened.'

'He didn't seem like the boys I date at home. They're always after sex, but I know how to treat them.'

'Men are the same the whole world over,' scoffed Kara. 'It's just that he seemed different because of his background. The island itself is enough to make any girl's thoughts turn to love.' Only by strictly controlling her own emotions could she stop herself falling in love with Aleko. She knew what she was talking about.

'I do love him,' declared Sharon. 'With all my heart.'

'But would you want to marry a man who didn't love you?'

'He says he loves me,' Sharon protested sulkily.

Kara wondered whether this was the right moment to tell her sister about the other girl. She thought not. She would wait a few more days. If Petros did decide to marry Sharon—if, it was a slim hope—then it would be best if she had not mentioned Katina.

'Has he told his family about you?'

'No.'

'He's afraid?'

'It's too soon,' defended Sharon.

'He's hoping it won't be necessary? He thinks it might be a false alarm?'

Sharon lifted her shoulders. 'I suppose so.'

'I think,' said Kara firmly, 'that you ought to get yourself off to a doctor.'

'And how can I do that without questions being asked?' demanded Sharon crossly. 'I'd have to go to Corfu, or the mainland. Can't you see how impossible that is? I'll go, when I'm ready, when I've sorted myself out with Petros. I wish you'd stop trying to organise my life!'

'I only want to help.' Kara eyed her sister angrily.

'I wish I hadn't told you.'

'So do I. What a hell of a mess to get into! Here of all places. I hate to think what Mum and Dad will say. They were so proud of you getting this job.'

Suddenly Sharon drew her feet out of the water, stood up, and dived cleanly into the pool. End of conversation, thought Kara bitterly, and went back indoors.

But she could not relax and in the end she decided to go for a walk. In the village the old men were still sitting at their tables outside the taverna. Did they ever do anything else? she wondered. Skinny cats snoozed in the dappled shade. An old woman sat on a stool weaving, nodding her head unsmilingly as Kara hurried past.

The Greeks had a completely different philosophy on life. There was no hustle and bustle. Everything was done at a leisurely pace and the clock was ignored. Kara's feet slowed. Why was she hurrying? Where was there to go? What was there to do? She turned and looked again at the old woman, watching her fingers deftly working the wool.

Eventually she arrived at the beach and sat with her knees drawn to her chin, looking out at the incredible blue of the sea. It was ironical that just as she had conditioned herself to having a good time with Aleko her sister had dropped this bombshell.

It would be difficult to hide her feelings. He would certainly guess there was something wrong. Should she tell him? Or wait until the news found its own way? Perhaps he already knew. With a heavy sigh she stripped down to her bikini and ran into the pellucid warm water.

How it soothed her! It was like silk caressing her skin, it washed all her troubles away. She dried off beneath the sun on her towel, then nibbled on the biscuits and apple she had brought with her.

Not until it was too hot for comfort did she wend her way back, stopping at the taverna for a long cold drink of lime juice, showering and throwing herself down naked on top of the bed the moment she reached the house.

She slept and dreamt of Aleko and woke feeling better, feeling excited about seeing him tonight, deciding in her mind what she would wear. Not the pink again, but a slinky white dress with a thread of silver running through it. It was not new, but it had been expensive and she knew she looked good in it.

And then surprisingly, long before the appointed hour, Aleko arrived. She was in her room and heard the roar of his car on the drive. With a happy smile she ran out to meet him. He couldn't even wait—he was as anxious as she.

Her heart thudded and her feet were light, but she came to an abrupt halt when she saw the grimness of his face. She had never seen such hostility. Muscles jerked in a taut jaw, his mouth was set in a straight angry line, and eyes as hard as bullets were fixed accusingly on her.

She swallowed hard and looked up at him, petrified by the force of his fury. All sorts of questions sprang to mind, but she could voice none. Her mouth hung open and she stood and looked, and waited, for whatever it was he had come to say, her heart pounding now from fear. He looked as though he was ready to commit murder.

'I want you to get off this island,' he grated through clenched teeth. 'I don't ever want to see you again.' He spoke slowly and distinctly, making sure she did not miss one single word.

Kara heard but did not understand. She frowned and started to speak, but Aleko silenced her with a glance.

'You and that damn sister of yours!'

Then she understood. 'Aleko, please——'

'I don't want to hear any explanations or excuses!' he roared. 'Just do as I say!' His fingers curled into fists and he swayed towards her. Kara thought he was going to hit her and she stepped back a pace, breathing hard, her mind racing frantically.

'I still have almost a week's holiday left,' she returned haughtily. 'I'm staying. And Sharon has her job. She won't leave either.'

His eyes narrowed until they were no more than black slits. 'It wouldn't be wise.'

'You don't intimidate me,' she thrust tightly.

'No?' He suddenly caught hold of her arms and shook

her. His fingers bit in hard and Kara knew she would be
bruised tomorrow. But she did not struggle. Instead she
held herself straight and tall and gazed into his eyes.

His nostrils flared and he bowed his head until his face
was only centimetres from hers. Still with his fingers
digging into her flesh, his nostrils flaring, his breath hot
on her cheeks, his eyes blazing, he said brutally, 'You're
a pair of scheming and conniving gold-diggers, and
don't try to deny it. But I must confess, I admire your
strategy. I was a fool not to see through you. Your little
game is over now, though.'

He kissed her hard and unexpectedly on the mouth,
his eyes glittering with hatred as he pulled away. 'One
last reminder of the temptress who almost brought me to
my knees.'

Then he wiped the back of his hand deliberately and
insolently across his mouth, throwing her such a look of
loathing and disgust that Kara felt physically sick.

She crossed her arms in front of her and rubbed her
bruised skin, shaking her head, her blue eyes clouded
and hurt. 'What is it I'm supposed to have done?'

'Oh, those pleading eyes! How many men have they
seduced?' He paused, and his hostility sliced through
the air like a rapier. 'And this——' He grabbed her left
hand and savagely twisted her wedding ring. 'This
symbol of—what? A marriage gone wrong? Am I still
expected to believe that?'

She thought he was going to wrench the ring off and
hurl it away, and she frantically tore at his fingers. This
was her barrier, her barrier against men such as he. 'Let
go of me, you maniac!'

'You're the one who's out of your mind,' rasped Aleko
harshly, crushing both her hands in one of his. 'What a
cunning plot you and your sister hatched—or was it her
idea? Is that why she got you out here? Two rich

bachelors—one each. Play your cards right and you'll never need to work again.'

'God, you swine!' cried Kara, wrestling free. 'Is that what you think?' Did he honestly believe she was after a rich husband? It was ludicrous!

'It's what I know,' he thrust between his teeth. His lips were thin, almost invisible, and the skin of his face was drawn tightly over his cheekbones.

'You've no basis for such an accusation,' she cried.

'No?'

'None.'

'I prefer to believe my own judgement,' he rasped.

'You don't think my sister is good enough for Petros, is that it?'

He took a deep steadying breath. 'You know that Petros is going to marry Katina?'

'They're thinking about it, yes,' she admitted. 'Thimios told me.'

'And it is a marriage which our mutual families approve. They are right for each other. This—this feeling Petros has for your sister—it is——' Aleko clicked his fingers in the air as if searching for the right words. 'It is no more than lust. A blonde is always an attraction—she is so different from our own girls—but she is for fun only. We prefer to marry our own.'

'Meaning,' said Kara, swallowing a sudden lump in her throat, 'that I meant nothing to you either. It was all a game.'

'That's right, a game,' he said brutally. 'A game that you started.'

He had given the impression earlier that he had begun to feel something for her. Or had she misinterpreted his statement? She did not think so. He said she had almost brought him to his knees. Was it pride now that made him retract his words? Not that she cared. Her emotions

were not involved, they never had been. Had they? She
wished she could truthfully answer that question.

'I seem to remember that you were the one who did
the chasing,' she said levelly.

'You let me think so. Your sex is, unfortunately, often
more clever than we give you credit for.'

Kara eyed him boldly. 'I'm not leaving. Nor is my
sister—not yet. Is there anything further you have to
say?'

For several seconds he held her gaze, breathing
deeply, his anger by no means lessened. 'For the
moment, no.' He swung on his heels, as correct as a
soldier, and marched to his car with his back ramrod-
straight. The engine roared and gravel spurted as he
surged furiously forward.

Long after he had disappeared from sight Kara could
still hear the angry revs of the engine, and as the
aftermath set in her legs began to tremble. How dared he
accuse her of pursuing him! Marriage to Aleko Tranakas
was the last thing she wanted. He was bigheaded and
conceited if he thought she would go to such lengths.

Still fuming, she made her way indoors, and had only
just closed her bedroom door when it opened again and
Sharon came in. Her sister's face was pale, her eyes wide
and frightened. 'What did Aleko want? I heard you
arguing. It wasn't about—me?'

How Kara wished she could squash her sister's fears,
but she had a strong feeling that Aleko had not finished
with them yet. He had got nowhere with her—but there
was still Sharon. And in her sister's present emotional
state she would be no match for him.

'The two of us,' she said, trying to smile. 'He's got
some bee in his bonnet that we're both after rich
husbands.'

'He thinks you're after him?' Sharon's eyebrows shot

up. 'He needs his head examining! You're the last person to want a man.'

'Thanks a lot,' said Kara indignantly, even though she knew her behaviour since Greg's death gave Sharon more than enough grounds for such a statement.

'You know what I mean,' said Sharon uncomfortably.

Kara grimaced. 'Unfortunately I changed my mind and decided I might as well enjoy myself.' Obviously her sister had not been listening when she told her about her experiences the other day.

'I see,' murmured Sharon, and then on a much stronger note, 'But how does he know about me? Petros said he wasn't going to say anything. Not yet. He's still hoping it might come to nothing.' Her eyes filled with tears.

'I've no idea how Aleko found out,' said Kara. 'All I can tell you is that he's in a hell of a mood about it. He wants us both off the island.'

Sharon's head jerked and her mouth grew suddenly mutinous. 'He can't do that! He doesn't own Lakades. I won't go—unless Petros comes with me.'

'Don't worry,' said Kara. 'I told him there was no chance. But I don't think we've heard the last. I'd like to meet Petros. Do you think you could arrange it?'

Sharon frowned. 'What for?'

'To talk some sense into him.'

Her sister shook her head vigorously, her flaxen hair flying, her wide blue-grey eyes horrified. 'I don't want you to interfere.'

'I wouldn't, if I didn't think it necessary,' said Kara quietly. 'But if he thinks he can get my sister pregnant and then just ditch her, he's mistaken.'

'I still don't think it's a good thing, you speaking to him.'

'No?' Kara raised her brows. 'You don't seem to be

getting anywhere yourself. When are you seeing him again?'

Sharon looked away, reluctant to commit herself. 'I have tomorrow afternoon off,' she mumbled. 'I was hoping to see him, but he's not sure whether he can get away.'

Kara speculated whether he had ever had any difficulty before? He sounded very immature. Could this be the reason he had discussed his problem with Aleko, knowing that he could not handle it himself? 'Is he coming here?' she asked.

'No.'

'So where are you meeting him—if he decides to turn up?' Kara could not hide her scepticism.

'At the beach,' came Sharon's reluctant admittance.

'I'll come with you.' Kara's tone was firm.

Sharon looked resentful but said no more, turning and trailing unhappily out of the room. Kara flung herself face-downwards on the bed, wondering what had happened to the relaxing holiday she had promised herself.

Dinner with the Hythes that evening was not easy. Sharon was absent, ostensibly keeping her eye on the twins, but Kara knew her own increasing anxiety over her sister was reflected in her face.

Fortunately Rosemary and Geoff put it down to the fact that her date with Aleko had yet again been cancelled. 'Aleko has some work to catch up on,' she had lied, that being the only logical explanation she could think of.

'How disappointed you must be,' said Rosemary. 'I was thrilled to see you getting on so well with him after all.'

Kara shrugged and tried to look unconcerned.

'That's the trouble when a man's so successful,'

persisted Rosemary. 'Duty comes before everything else. But if my instinct's correct I think he'll still keep in touch after you've returned to England.'

'What a turn-up for the books it would be if you were the one to hook him,' chortled Geoff. 'From what I hear there are many who've tried. He's certainly some catch.'

Kara shook her head. 'There's nothing like that between us. It was just a mild flirtation on Aleko's part. In fact,' she laughed lightly, 'I think he's tired of me already.'

'Kara!' cried Rosemary. 'Don't say that.'

Twisting her lips wryly, Kara said, 'We'll see.'

Before she went to bed she popped her head round Sharon's door, but her sister was asleep, or pretending to be, and she did not disturb her.

Kara could not sleep, however. She lay awake for hours and hours worrying. Would she be doing the right thing by interfering? Would it not be best to let them sort out their own problems? They were both old enough—Sharon was twenty and Petros a year or two older. Sharon had said that he loved her—and she obviously was very much in love with him. So surely, given time, he would come to his senses?

But time was something Kara did not have a lot of. And she could not go back to England without knowing what was happening. Was it Katina he truly loved? If so, she must make him tell the truth, however much it hurt Sharon.

Thoughts of Aleko too filled her troubled mind. It hurt more than she cared to admit that he should believe they were both scheming gold-diggers. In one way she could understand why he thought it of Sharon, but that he should assume she, Kara, had deliberately set her sights on him because of his wealth, was the worst insult he could have paid her. Her blood boiled and she

thought of all the things she could have said to him, and
hadn't. Heavens, he was the last man she would wish to
get deeply involved with!

Why then did she feel as much upset as angry? Surely
it didn't matter what he thought of her? It was the
unfairness of it all that counted. But deep down inside
she knew it was more than that. She had become too
fond of him, no matter what she tried to tell herself.
Whether she was actually in love was debatable, but she
was on the very brink—and it would have been so easy to
fall over the edge. 'Damn!' she said angrily to herself.
'Damn, damn, damn.'

Sharon avoided her the next morning by taking the
twins on a long nature walk; nevertheless Kara intended
making sure her sister did not leave without her to meet
Petros. Rosemary was not at work and had planned a
further excursion for Amanda and Damien after their
usual nap, so as soon as Sharon had settled them Kara
confronted her.

'I'm ready when you are,' she said with attempted
brightness.

Sharon shrugged, her face sulky, and as they walked
through the village to the beach the atmosphere between
them was the most uncomfortable Kara had ever
experienced.

'I don't think he'll come,' said Sharon. 'You're
wasting your time.'

'In which case I'll be company for you,' replied Kara
reasonably.

'I don't want company.'

Kara shook her head in despair. 'If he doesn't turn up
then he'll go down even further in my estimation.'

Sharon's eyes flashed hotly. 'You're prejudiced
because we've spoilt your chances with Aleko.'

'Don't be ridiculous!' snapped Kara. 'I never fancied

Aleko, not one little bit. What a stupid thing to say! He
was company, that's all.' She knew she was protesting
too strongly. 'I never planned for anything to come of it.
I came out here to see you and then discovered that—
somehow—you couldn't find time for me. What did you
expect me to do, sit and twiddle my thumbs?'

'I didn't want you to find out what was wrong,'
admitted Sharon sullenly. 'But it got too much when
Petros took the attitude he did. I couldn't keep it to
myself any longer.'

And then they reached the beach—and there was
Petros. He wore nothing but swimming trunks and
sandals. He was young and he looked strong. He was
incredibly handsome and there was a vitality about him
that made even Kara realise what it was that had
attracted Sharon.

She looked at her sister and saw the love shining in her
eyes, and vowed in that moment to do all she could to
help.

CHAPTER SIX

WHEN Petros saw Sharon was not alone he looked taken aback, his eyes darting swiftly from one to the other, finally coming to rest questioningly on the younger girl.

'This is my sister Kara.' Sharon's tone was apologetic. 'She wanted to meet you. Kara, this is Petros,' she added unnecessarily.

Kara held out her hand and warily he took it. 'I am pleased to make your acquaintance,' he said in very correct English.

'So you are Petros.' Kara looked at him unsmilingly. What beautiful eyes he had! Dark and large and thickly lashed. His body was thin and wiry, but hard and deeply tanned. When he was Aleko's age, when he had broadened out, matured a little, he would be even more devastating than his half-brother. He would break many a heart. 'I can see now why Sharon has fallen in love with you.'

He looked embarrassed, as Kara intended he should. She needed to be in control of the situation. 'Do you love my sister?' she asked abruptly.

Petros glanced at Sharon who was glaring furiously at Kara. 'Yes,' he sounded cautious, as if a little unsure of himself, 'of course I love her.'

Kara was not entirely convinced, though Sharon seemed satisfied enough, smiling at the boy and moving closer towards him, throwing her sister a defensive look which said, 'I told you so'.

He put his arm about her shoulders and she put hers around his waist. They were much the same height, and

Sharon's nearly-white hair was a startling contrast to the raven blackness of his. They made a striking couple, and Kara could not help feeling it was a pity circumstances were not different.

'And what are you going to do about this baby she's expecting?' continued Kara, deciding to plunge right in while she had the advantage.

He lowered his eyes and his Adam's apple went up and down several times as he swallowed nervously. The fact that he could find no words gave her the answer she was seeking. 'Why did you go to see Aleko?' she demanded next. 'What did you hope he would do?'

'Take no notice of her!' shrieked Sharon, close to tears. 'She's just angry because we've spiked her affair with him!'

'Spiked?' Petros frowned. 'I do not understand. What is spiked?'

'Put a stop to it. Ruined it!' cried Sharon. The girl sounded almost hysterical, and Kara felt like shaking her.

'I am sorry,' said Petros, 'if that has happened. It was not my fault. Aleko overheard me and Sharon talking— we were not careful. He was very cross. He said I was to leave the matter with him and he would deal with it.' The boy's cheeks flushed, but he looked directly at Kara and she knew that he spoke the truth.

'I think, Petros,' she said quietly, 'that you and I ought to have a few words alone.' She felt so much older and wiser than he, yet there could be no more than a year or two between them.

'Why?' demanded Sharon at once, hanging on to his arm as though she was afraid her sister might be after Petros herself.

'I need to talk to him without you butting in after every sentence,' said Kara firmly. 'Petros?'

He looked at her doubtfully, then with a shrug he prised Sharon away. 'Go for a swim,' he said gently. 'In a minute I will join you.'

Her mouth was set in that mutinous line Kara was beginning to know so well. 'But, Petros——'

'Please,' he said, kissing her cheek lightly.

Sharon looked into his eyes and saw that he meant it. With a venomous glare at Kara she stepped out of her shorts, revealing a daringly minuscule bikini, and stalked away down the beach.

Petros gazed after her, openly admiring the graceful movements of her body. She was tall and willowy and her stomach was still firm and flat. Was it any wonder he was taken with her?

Kara watched him and saw the desire in his eyes. But if he was merely playing with her sister then he had better look out.

Finally he looked back at Kara. He had been unaware she was observing him and he quickly lowered his lids, shifting uncomfortably.

'My sister's a beautiful girl,' she commented. 'But are you sure that it's love you feel for her?'

'Why do you ask me—again?' he questioned defensively.

'Because,' returned Kara slowly, 'I know about Katina.'

His eyes widened with shock and his mouth fell open. 'How did you find out?' he asked hoarsely. 'Does Sharon know?'

'No, I've said nothing to my sister,' replied Kara.

Petros looked faintly relieved. 'Did Aleko tell you?'

Kara shook her head. 'Katina herself told me about you when I went visiting with Aleko. What I didn't know then was that it was you Sharon was seeing. She never mentioned your name until—until she told me about the baby. What are you going to do about it?'

He scuffed a toe in the sand, looking anywhere except at Kara. 'Aleko insists that there is not one. He claims that Sharon is trying to force me to marry her.'

Kara's nostrils dilated and she stared at him accusingly. 'And do you believe she is lying?'

He swallowed hard. 'I—I do not know what to think. She has not seen a doctor. She——'

Anger filled Kara. 'We both know how difficult that is. What are you trying to say, Petros? That if she's not pregnant you won't marry her? That in fact you don't love her at all? That you never have. You merely wanted an affair with no strings attached?' She was breathing hard by the time she had finished. How these Tranakas men infuriated her!

'Aleko wants me to marry Katina,' Petros said quietly.

'Then show that you're a man and make a stand, for heaven's sake! Aleko's merely trying to frighten you. It's your life, Petros. Sharon loves you very much, so much that you're breaking her heart. And if you love her then for God's sake don't let Aleko ruin things between you.'

'There are still my parents,' he continued worriedly.

'Who will understand, I'm sure, once you explain. Be strong, Petros. You can't let other people run your life—unless you really don't love my sister? I don't want you to marry her if that's the case. It wouldn't work.'

He glanced at her anxiously from beneath thick black lashes. 'I love her. But Katina—I love her too. Is that possible?'

Kara groaned inwardly. 'You can't love them both in exactly the same manner. You've known Katina a long time. Perhaps it's brotherly love you feel for her?'

He lifted his shoulders. 'I did not think so before I met Sharon.'

'Then you have a great deal of thinking to do. If you

must let my sister down, Petros, then do it for all the
right reasons, not because Aleko insists on it. Make up
your own mind. It's your life that's at stake.'

'You are very understanding,' he said. 'I am sorry if I
cause you a lot of worry.'

'It's Sharon who worries me,' she sighed, glancing at
the sparkling ocean. 'This is the first time she's been
away from home for any length of time. She assured us
she could look after herself.'

He grimaced. 'And you are saying that I treat her
badly?'

'You could have been more careful.' Her eyes scanned
the water. 'Especially if you weren't serious.' Where was
Sharon? There were only two or three other groups of
people on the beach and none were swimming.

'You are accusing me?' he asked reproachfully.

'Both of you,' she snapped, walking past him to the
water's edge, her eyes narrowed as she continued to
search for her sister.

Petros followed, and she felt him go tense as he too
looked for Sharon. The sea was rougher than it had
been, the waves breaking in white foam on the shore.
Kara had not felt the wind get up, now she feared for
Sharon's safety. Perhaps, she thought hopefully, her
sister had got fed up with swimming, and gone for a
walk. Kara turned and shading her eyes scanned the
surrounding area. But Sharon was nowhere in sight.

And then from out to sea they heard a faint yell. Petros
saw her first and he kicked off his sandals, charging into
the water like a man demented, striking out as soon as it
was deep enough to swim.

Sharon was a long way out, much further than they
had been looking, her head no more than a tiny dot. She
was not an exceptionally strong swimmer, and Kara
wondered how she had managed to get that far. She

watched anxiously as her sister sometimes disappeared altogether, hidden by the rolling waves. Please God, let Petros save her, she prayed silently.

The other groups of people had all walked to the water's edge and were watching and praying too. Kara heard them talking among themselves and acknowledged their words of comfort.

Petros was, she noticed thankfully, making rapid progress through the water. She watched as the gap closed between them, urging Sharon to hang on, almost crying in despair when her sister's head disappeared for over a minute.

And then there were two heads together, and they drew nearer and nearer, and finally, after what seemed a lifetime, they were close enough for her to wade in and help Petros pull her sister out.

Sharon collapsed white-faced and choking on to the sand, but she was conscious and her eyes flickered over Kara. 'I'm sorry,' she whispered.

Sorry? For what? Had she done it deliberately? Had she tried to take her own life? Or was she sorry for the worry she had caused? At the moment it did not matter.

Petros's breathing was ragged, but he stood tall, his hands on his hips, his chest heaving. 'I have my car,' he said. 'I will take Sharon home.'

Kara nodded, conscious only of relief that her sister was still alive. He lifted Sharon easily into his arms and they trekked across the sand. Kara spread a blanket on the back seat and he laid her on it.

It was a short journey, and by the time they reached the Hythes' house Sharon was sitting and looked almost her normal self.

'Thank you, Petros, for saving me,' she whispered huskily, her eyes full of tears.

'I couldn't let you drown,' he said tensely.

'It might have been best.'

He groaned and crushed her to him, and Kara walked away. They needed a few minutes together.

When Petros finally left and Sharon came into the house Kara had a hot bath ready. Her sister was subdued, but seemed none the worse for her experience, though Kara decided to leave her questions for the moment.

Rosemary returned with the twins and Sharon begged her sister to say nothing. 'I'm fine now, there's no point in worrying her.'

'All right,' agreed Kara, 'but I want a word with you later. It was a very foolish thing to do and——'

Her words were cut short when Amanda and Damien raced up to them, their faces alight with excitement. 'Sharon, guess where we've been!'

Kara stayed for a minute or two, then went out into the garden and sat by the pool. It was peaceful here. She closed her eyes and listened to the birds and the silence.

Her thoughts inevitably turned to Aleko and she found it difficult to believe that the same person who had sent her soaring to the heights and stripped her body of its defences had ordered her to leave the island. How could he change so abruptly? How could he believe it had all been a game? And how dared he say her sister was lying!

She had to see him. She could not allow him to go on thinking the worst; she must set the matter straight. But when? Maybe she could go to the Tranakas villa tonight? She ought to have asked Petros whether his half-brother would be in. It was a long way to go for a wasted journey. Perhaps if she phoned first? But that would forewarn him, and she did not wish to give Aleko time to prepare his arguments.

She was still wrestling with her problem when Geoff

came home and it was time to change for dinner. Afterwards the Hythes insisted she join them for a game of cards, so all hopes of going out that evening were dashed.

Nor did she see Sharon again. Once the twins were in bed her sister shut herself in her room and locked the door, not even answering when Kara knocked.

The next morning Sharon and the twins had gone off somewhere before Kara got up—an event so unusual that Kara knew it was deliberate. Rosemary was working a whole day at the office, so Kara had the house to herself.

She toyed with the idea of ringing Aleko and asking him to come and see her, and several times actually picked up the phone and dialled his office number, but always replaced it before anyone answered.

Later she went for a swim, and when she climbed out of the pool there was no longer any need to try and contact him, for he was there. He wore grey slacks and a white shirt with a dark tie, the knot slackened, his shirt collar unbuttoned. His face was as hard and implacable as it had been the last time she saw him.

It was difficult trying to look dignified wearing a bikini, nevertheless Kara stood tall, holding her head high, hoping the pounding of her heart did not show. She decided to go straight into the attack.

'How dare you insinuate that my sister is lying!' she gritted through her teeth. 'What a despicable thing to suggest—without evidence too! I demand that you apologise.'

Black brows rose arrogantly and he looked down his nose at her as though she were a nobody. Not the girl he had spent a night with. Not the girl he had whispered words of love to. Nobody—an intruder, a nuisance. 'She isn't the first girl to try it, and she won't be the last,' he said. 'Petros and I are used to such allegations.'

'Petros happens to believe her,' Kara snapped.

'Would she truly try to take her own life if she were expecting his child?'

Kara felt a moment's shock, then her head jerked. 'Would she truly try to take her own life if she wasn't? I presume you've been speaking to Petros? But whatever he's told you it's not true. Sharon simply swam further than she intended She's a sane, rational girl and would never attempt such a thing.'

Mentally she crossed her fingers that this was the truth. The Sharon she had grown up with would certainly never have done such a thing, but in her present frame of mind anything was possible.

'No sane, rational girl, as you put it,' Aleko commented tersely, 'would try to blackmail a man into marrying her.'

'My sister is not blackmailing Petros!'

'That is your opinion.'

'It's the truth.'

'In your eyes only. I happen to think differently. Tell me, why has she not arranged to see a doctor?'

'Because,' she cried furiously, 'she didn't want anyone to know until she had told Petros.' She realised he would think this a feeble excuse, but it was the truth, whether he believed it or not.

'So——' he said arrogantly, 'she has now told him. There are no further excuses. If she provides proof, then so be it. Until then I have forbidden Petros to see her.'

Kara gasped. 'Who the hell do you think you are—his keeper? My God, Aleko, I can't believe it! Do you really think you can keep them apart, if they want to see each other?'

'He will do as I say.' His eyes rested coldly on her, his tone confident. 'We will see who is right.'

'And is that why you've come here today?' she spat.
'To make sure my sister gets the message, loud and
clear?'

'To make sure you both get the message,' he clipped
tautly. 'You are no different from your sister. Different
tactics, but with the same end in mind.'

Her eyes blazed. 'I wouldn't marry you, Aleko
Tranakas, if you paid me a million pounds. What a
conceit! The thought never even crossed my mind.' A
lie—it had occurred to her, but not now, not any longer.
He was the most arrogant, despicable man she had ever
met. She shook her head in pure bewilderment.

His eyes narrowed and he clearly disbelieved her. She
expected another comeback and was surprised when he
said coldly, 'Actually there is another reason why I am
here. To pass on my parents' invitation for you and
Sharon to join us for dinner—tonight.'

Kara's chin shot up and she eyed him suspiciously.
'Why? Do they want to see for themselves what the two
mercenary sisters look like?'

'They don't know what you're up to,' he rasped.
'They simply thought it would make a change—for you
both. But they were especially concerned about you
since I'd had to cancel my earlier invitations.'

'I assume you didn't tell them why the second one was
withdrawn?' she asked icily.

'No,' he admitted, 'I didn't. But my father and
Sophia, that's my stepmother, are good kind generous
people, and I don't want them hurt. So you will accept,
and you will say nothing of my wishes for you to leave.'

Her fine brows arched. 'Do you really think I'll be able
to pretend there's nothing wrong? You might be a good
actor, Aleko, but I can assure you I'm not. I couldn't
possibly be civil to you, not now.'

'Then perhaps,' he mused, 'for a few hours we ought

to call a truce?' He caught her wrist and pulled her hard against him, and when his head lowered to hers Kara was too stunned by his duplicity to stop him.

He held nothing back, moving his lips gently and erotically over hers, tempting her to respond, persuading her that the physical attraction they both felt had in no way diminished.

Beneath her hand she felt the quickened beat of his heart, and his body hardened in arousal as hips and thighs welded together. Kara trembled and moved even closer against him, her lips clinging now to his, unable to stem the tide of desire that washed over her.

His mouth moved down her throat and he urged a thigh between hers, and Kara cursed the coarse material of his trousers, preferring his hair-roughened skin.

A low moan escaped her arched throat as his mouth moved even lower, nudging away the scrap of material covering her breasts, gently biting, tormenting, inciting.

'Oh, Aleko,' she heard herself say.

'It is good for you?' His eyes were narrowed, his voice low.

She groaned. 'Very good. I don't know why you do this to me, but you do.'

'When two people are as compatible as we there can be no holding back.'

Sexually compatible, that was what he meant. That was all there ever could be between them. He despised her as a person, but he could not deny the needs of his own body. Nor could she. Her loins throbbed with an aching hunger for him, and her hands tugged his shirt free so that she could slide her fingers over the smooth hardness of his back.

The sensual delight in touching this man was such as she had never experienced before. She wanted more and more of him. She could not get enough. She wanted to feel every intimate place as she had that night she spent in his bed. She wanted him to do the same to her.

Forgotten was the fact that he was trying to throw her off the island. All sane thoughts had fled. Their bodies fitted together like two pieces of a jigsaw puzzle.

With the same consideration he had used to start their lovemaking Aleko slowed the pace and finally stopped altogether, still holding her but his mouth and hands making no demands.

Kara looked up at him, her parted lips soft and slightly swollen, her eyes shining, her breathing ragged. Her mouth felt dry and her whole body throbbed, and his powers of persuasion could not be denied.

She would go tonight with the remembrance of these moments still warm inside her. One look out of those deeply sensual eyes and she would melt. She would not need to act. He held her in the palm of his hand—and he knew it.

She ran the tip of her tongue across her lips and leaned against him. 'Will Petros be there?' she asked huskily.

Aleko shook his head.

'Then I don't think Sharon will come either.'

'So don't tell her.' He stroked her bikini top back into place and Kara's breathing quickened again.

'Is that fair?'

'It's my parents' party. What can I do about it?'

'Nothing, I suppose,' she shrugged, knowing that even if he could arrange it he would make no attempt.

'But just make sure your sister comes.' There was the merest hardening to his tone, but it was accompanied by a persuasive smile and Kara knew she would do as he said. She was completely under his spell.

'What do we wear?' she asked softly.

His eyes met hers. 'Whatever you think will please me.

And now I must go.' His hand cupped her chin. 'Think you can survive until you see me again?'

'I might just manage it,' she said, responding to his teasing tone.

He lowered his head and brushed his lips across hers. 'Till tonight, then. I shall look forward to it. It should be quite an occasion.'

Kara watched as he walked away, his stride relaxed and long, just the slightest swagger to his hips. He was tucking his shirt into his pants as he disappeared from sight, and seconds later she heard the engine leap into life, and the soft purr as he rolled his car out of the drive.

She was amazed by her own weakness. She ought really to have put her foot down and followed her first instinctive refusal. But it was done now and it would probably be quite a pleasant evening. Besides, it would be interesting to see what Aleko's father was like. Would he be an older version of his son? Or would there be no resemblance at all?

When Sharon returned at lunchtime Kara told her of the invitation. Sharon looked surprised but also pleased. 'If it means I'll see Petros then of course I'll go,' she said happily. 'I wonder what made them ask?'

'Apparently they thought we might enjoy the change.'

'What does Aleko think about the invitation?'

Kara shrugged. 'He's prepared to call a temporary truce. He doesn't want to upset his parents.'

'Think you can manage it?' asked Sharon archly.

Kara nodded, conscious of a sudden flush of warmth at the thought of seeing Aleko again tonight.

Sharon would have walked away, but Kara called her back. 'You've not said how you're feeling. No after-effects? No harm done? I could swear you've been avoiding me?'

Her sister shrugged and smiled self-consciously. 'Why should I? I'm fine.'

'Why did you do it?'

Sharon frowned.

'Try to drown yourself,' Kara explained.

'Is that what you think?'

'It's what it looked like.'

'Would I have shouted for help if I wanted to end my life?'

Kara shrugged. 'I suppose not. But you could easily have drowned. What made you go out so far?' She was not convinced. Sharon had been living on her nerves ever since she got here; it was just possible that she could have tried to put an end to her unhappiness.

'I didn't realise the sea had got so rough,' explained Sharon. 'It took me out further than I intended.'

Kara was compelled to accept her explanation. 'You're lucky he's a strong swimmer,' she told her.

'I know. He was pretty fantastic, wasn't he?' Sharon's eyes lit up with an inner radiance as she walked away.

Kara dressed carefully for the dinner party in a straight cream skirt, that had the look of linen yet was fashioned from an uncrushable man-made fibre, teaming it with a camisole top that she had crocheted herself in the long evenings after Greg's death.

She applied make-up carefully, not too much to give the wrong impression, yet sufficient to enlarge her blue eyes, her lids shimmering with ice-blue shadow, her cheekbones accented with blusher, her lips frosted with pale-pink lipstick.

There was nothing she could do with her hair. Cropped as short as it was, there was one style only for it, but with it freshly shampooed and teased into feathery fronds about her face, she felt as good as the image reflected in her mirror.

She had never looked prettier, she thought, standing this way and that and surveying herself critically. She had bloomed these last few days. Her holiday really was doing her good. Or was it Aleko?

Her lips lifted as she thought about him and a warm glow enveloped her. She was looking forward to seeing him tonight. Tomorrow he would again be the autocrat demanding their departure. But she would not think about that. She would forget everything except that he was the man she was in danger of falling in love with.

Aleko sent a car for them, driven by an impassive-faced Greek who remained silent for the whole of the journey.

Sharon was very excited, sitting on the edge of her seat, her wide eyes brilliant with pleasure. 'I wonder if Petros has told his parents about me? Perhaps that's one of the reasons they've invited us to dinner?'

Kara dared not dampen her sister's enthusiasm, but wished it were possible for her to show her own feelings so openly. She had to remember that this was a temporary truce, that she meant nothing to Aleko. She was a toy for him to toss around at his will, and try as she might she had not the strength to resist him.

CHAPTER SEVEN

THE TRANAKAS villa was even more imposing at close quarters than it had looked from Kara's bedroom window. She decided it reminded her of the Achilleon Palace in Corfu with its Moorish-type arches, its terraces overlooking the bay, its stone balustrades and winding steps. It was magnificent and far too grand to be just a family home. It looked as though it should belong to royalty at the very least.

After passing between black and gold wrought iron gates, which had opened automatically as the car approached, they followed a curving drive through terraced gardens which were a riot of colour, each turn bringing the house nearer, each bend revealing more and more of this unbelievably beautiful place.

'Isn't it fantastic!' cried Sharon, sitting on the edge of the seat, her eyes alight with interest and curiosity. 'Fancy living somewhere like this. Isn't it out of this world?'

Kara nodded, equally impressed, but not as given to showing her feelings as her sister.

When the car stopped Sharon jumped out before the chauffeur could open the door, looking about her with eyes as wide as saucers. Kara hated to think what would happen to this bubble of happiness when she discovered that Petros was not here, and she silently prayed that Sharon would not show her hurt too much.

Half expecting a servant to open the massive oak door, Kara was surprised when Aleko himself appeared on the steps. His wide smile embraced them both and Kara felt the now familiar warmth spread through her veins. She grew as excited as a kitten with a ball of wool and she knew it shone from her eyes. There was not a thing she could do about it either. She and Sharon were ensnared by these Tranakas men.

Her sister's eyes moved beyond Aleko, clearly hoping to see Petros, and Kara saw her swift moue of disappointment. But it was quickly replaced by a smile and the girl ran up the steps to her lover's brother. 'Hello, Aleko.' She seemed to have forgotten that he did not approve of her.

'Sharon. Kara.' He looked over the top of the younger girl's head and his smile was for Kara alone. Her legs threatened to buckle beneath her and she could not take her eyes off his as she mounted the steps to his side.

He lifted her chin with a warm firm finger and brushed her lips with his, but light though the touch was it seared her. Had she not known that tonight was a charade it would be so easy to believe she really meant something to him. What an accomplished actor he was!

They moved through into the entrance hall, which was circular and high with a mosaic floor in a Greek key pattern, the walls covered in gold wallpaper and hung with pictures that looked like originals.

A curved marble staircase branched upwards from each side and the balustrade along the gallery was made from marble too. A huge central chandelier spilled glittering teardrops of crystal, and Kara imagined how beautiful it would look when lit.

Sharon whirled round and round, her head dropped back on her shoulders, feasting her eyes on the ornately painted ceiling. It reminded Kara of the Sistine Chapel, and she wondered who had painted it.

'If you'd like to come this way?'

Their attention reclaimed, Aleko led them into an immense room where their eyes were immediately drawn to the deep wide windows at the other end. They opened out on to a balcony and provided a tantalising glimpse of the impossibly blue bay. The curtains were in deep blue brocade, and the several sofas and armchairs set about the room were covered to match. The rugs on the marble floor were in blue and gold and there was an antique chiffonier and several occasional tables. Again there was a crystal chandelier, and the ceiling was decorated with superb plaster mouldings.

Kara could not imagine anyone living here. It was like a show-place, the sort of home where one paid money to look around. 'Please sit down,' Aleko invited. 'I'll tell my parents that you've arrived.'

'I wonder where Petros is?' mused Sharon the moment they were alone. 'I expected him to be here to meet me.'

Deciding silence was the best policy, Kara pretended an interest in a sculpted marble table-lighter, testing it to see if it worked, her head jerking backwards when the flame almost singed her eyebrows.

And the next moment Aleko returned. Nikolaos Tranakas was, as she had predicted, an older version of Aleko—the same height and breadth, the same thick hair, except that his father's was almost white, the same strong features and jutting brows. His tanned face was lined, his mouth slightly weary, but he was a stunning man still and Kara liked him on sight.

His grip was firm and sincere. 'Welcome to my house, Kara. I've been looking forward to meeting you. Aleko has told us much about you.'

Kara flickered a swift frown in Aleko's direction, but

he was not looking at her. Instead he was saying something softly to his stepmother.

The next moment he introduced her to Kara. Sophia was short and plump and her still-black hair was drawn back from her face in a chignon. She smiled warmly and pumped Kara's hand, reiterating her husband's greeting. 'We do not often have visitors, except on business. It is a great pleasure to have someone from England. The Hythes are making you welcome, I hope?'

Kara smiled and murmured something appropriate, standing back and watching Aleko as he introduced her younger sister, mentally crossing her fingers that Sharon would not ask where Petros was.

Aleko was wearing cream trousers that moulded themselves sexily to his slim hips and muscular thighs. His black shirt was open at the throat, the cuffs folded back to reveal tough sinewy arms. His jaw was freshly shaven and his hair still damp and he looked devastating and virile, and Kara could not take her eyes off him.

Conscious of her appraisal, he slanted her several deliberately sensual glances, setting her pulses racing, and bringing a responsive smile to her lips. He was certainly making sure that she would not let him down!

By the time the introductions were over her heart was thudding fit to burst and the whole evening was taking on an importance it did not deserve.

They sat out on the balcony and Aleko poured aperitifs. Sharon drank hers quickly and nervously, constantly looking over her shoulder, obviously wondering what it was that kept Petros so long.

Any minute she would realise he was not at home, thought Kara, and it was unlikely her sister would be able to keep her unhappiness to herself. What had made Aleko invite her?

Sophia was speaking to Sharon. 'The twins, Amanda and Damien, they are a handful, are they not?'

'Sometimes,' nodded Sharon, 'but I love children.'

'Geoff and Rosemary brought them here, when they first came to the island. They exhausted me. And Nikolaos—he disappeared altogether.' Sophia's black eyes rested lovingly on her husband. 'I think we are too old. We love our own boys, naturally, but we are glad they are grown up.'

'One day you'll have grandchildren,' said Sharon.

Kara held her breath. Surely her sister wasn't testing the ground?

Sophia looked at her stepson and smiled fondly. 'One day, yes, I expect so. Indeed I hope so. But it is different when they are your own. Do you not agree?'

Sharon nodded emphatically. 'I'd like a large family. I think——'

'And I think we ought to discuss something other than babies,' put in Aleko firmly, frowning at Sharon, warning her that he did not approve of the way the conversation was going.

'It is perfectly natural she should talk about them,' reproved Sophia. 'After all, it is her job, looking after children. She adores them.'

'Am *I* talking about wine?' he questioned sharply, though with a beguiling smile which Kara guessed always won him his own way. Sophia might not be his natural mother, but there was certainly a bond between them and she could not be any more fond of him.

'You are not,' said his father, 'but it is unusual. I think, son, that we are outnumbered by these beautiful ladies.'

'I think we should go and eat,' smiled Aleko, offering his arm to Sophia. Nikolaos instantly and gallantly offered each of his arms to the Lincroft girls, beaming like a Cheshire Cat as he escorted them through to the dining room.

As Kara had known would be the case, the table was set for five only. She glanced at her sister and saw the dismay in her eyes, but she also saw Sharon lift her chin and firm her lips, and knew there would be no questions asked. Good for you, Sharon, she mentally praised.

The room was elegant with pink satin wallpaper and dull green rugs. The oval redwood table was set with sparkling crystal, shining silver and crisp damask napkins. A bowl of heavily scented roses sat in the centre and at either end were pink candles already lit.

The shuttered windows filtered the daylight, the room was cool and welcoming, and Kara was entranced.

'How nice of you to have gone to all this trouble,' she said to Sophia. 'We do appreciate you inviting us. I'd often wondered what your house was like inside. I can see it from my window at the Hythes. It's very impressive.'

'You must get Aleko to show you around later.' The woman looked pleased by the compliment. 'Actually it was his——'

'Do sit down, Kara.' His voice close to her ear drowned the rest of Sophia's sentence. His hand on her arm guided her to one of the chairs.

Tiny shock waves went through her at his touch, and when his fingers lingered over-long on the bare flesh of her shoulders, she wanted nothing more than to lift her face for his kiss. Her whole body was beginning to ache for him and she knew that the next few hours would be torture.

Would he show her around later, as his mother had suggested? Would they get some time on their own? Or would the charade end once there was no one to impress? Would he once again turn into the hostile stranger who wanted them off the island? She could not believe that it was all an act. He must still feel something for her, despite his harsh accusations. Perhaps he would change his mind? Perhaps tonight would prove to him that they were not the scheming sisters he thought?

As he took his seat at the opposite side of the table his eyes were still on hers, and how she wished it was just the two of them. He was inciting her to fever-pitch, if he only knew it.

'How much longer before you return to England?'

Kara suddenly realised that Aleko's father was speaking to her, and it was a real effort to drag her attention back to the present company. Nikolaos was sitting next to her, and on the other side of the table Aleko was flanked by Sharon and Sophia. 'I'm sorry,' she managed to stammer, 'I was miles away. A few more days, that's all. I fly back on Sunday.'

'I trust you have enjoyed your stay on our beautiful island?'

'Indeed I have,' she smiled. 'It's very—very different from England.' She had been about to say tranquil. But Aleko had succeeded in ruining the peace she had found. In more ways than one!

She nibbled at the stuffed vine-leaf that a silent-footed servant had placed in front of her. It was good, the meat and rice cooked to perfection, the creamy cheese sauce enhancing its flavour.

'It is many years since I have been in England,' commented Nickolaos. 'In fact I met Sophia there, she was visiting her English grandmother, so it holds happy memories. Aleko and Petros, they go there often, but me, I am too old for much travelling.'

Kara judged him to be in his sixties, which certainly did not make him senile. But she guessed he was contented here in this fine house.

She caught Sharon's eye. Her sister had heard Petros's name mentioned and was listening to see if any more was said.

'Have you been to the Greek islands before?' persisted the older man.

Kara nodded. 'Once.'

Perhaps it was the tone of her voice that made Nikolaos look at her sharply. 'It was not a happy occasion? Where did you go?'

'Corfu, and it was entirely happy, thank you. It was my honeymoon.' At that stage she had been besotted by Greg and the whole holiday had taken on a magical air.

'Oh, I am sorry,' he said at once. 'Aleko told us you were a widow. I know how painful such memories can be. I still sometimes get upset when I think about my first wife, and that was a long time ago. I loved her dearly. You have my sympathy, Kara. But you are young, there will be other men.'

Was it an accident that he glanced across at Aleko? Did he think that she might be falling for his elder son? Was she so transparent? And would he approve of such a relationship? She gave an inward bitter smile. If only he knew what Aleko really thought!

Wine was poured and conversation was passed back and forth. Their plates were cleared and a great dish of steaming moussaka placed in front of them. Kara noticed that Sharon only toyed with her food.

'It is a pity,' said Sophia suddenly, her cheeks glowing as she finished her third glass of wine, her smile growing wider by the minute, 'that Petros is not here. I don't like odd numbers.'

Kara saw Sharon's faint nod of agreement.

'But I know he would not have joined us even had I asked him,' continued their hostess, unconscious of the interest she had aroused in her young guest. 'Love comes first when you are young, and he has not seen Katina for——' she waved her hands expressively, 'for a long, long time. Aleko, you bad boy, you work him too hard.'

'How else will he learn the business?' asked Aleko smoothly. His eyes were unfathomable as they met Kara's. She had no idea what was going through his mind.

'And then you give him this time off just when I am having my dinner party. Could you not have arranged it better?'

'You should have told me earlier,' smiled Aleko easily. 'I know as well as you that once Petros has arranged to see Katina nothing or no one will stop him.'

Nikolaos smiled broadly. 'They are so in love, those two. They are childhood sweethearts, did you know?' He looked at Kara and Sharon collectively. 'We are expecting any day now to hear when they want to get married.'

The stem of Sharon's wine glass snapped and her face went paper-white. Kara caught the hint of Aleko's satisfied smile and in that instant knew.

He had arranged all this. He had done it deliberately, knowing full well that during the course of the evening the truth was sure to come out. She felt sick. What a devious, cunning swine he was! What a clever way of getting rid of her sister.

'Sharon, are you all right?' She glanced at the girl's stricken face, silently damning Aleko for doing this to her.

With superb self-control her sister flickered her eyes over the seated company. 'I'm sorry, I must have held the glass too tightly. I didn't realise it was so fragile. I hope it wasn't irreplaceable?'

'Do not worry about the glass,' said Sophia at once. 'Is your hand all right? You haven't cut it?'

Sharon shook her head.

'You look very pale,' commented Nikolaos. 'Are you not feeling well? I notice you have not eaten very much. Would you like to lie down?'

'I'll be all right,' insisted Sharon, glancing at Kara, mutely appealing for help.

'I think perhaps we should go home,' she said apologetically.

'Surely not yet?' pleaded Sophia anxiously. 'I was so enjoying your company. Let's go out on to the balcony and have coffee. It's very stuffy in here. Perhaps that's what's wrong?'

Aleko looked pleased that the evening was not being cut short. Kara guessed he wanted to prolong Sharon's agony. He really was cruel.

'Let me help you, Sharon.' He stood up and offered her his arm, and Kara wished her sister knew what he had done so that she could spit in his eye. But he was all charm and concern, and in no time they were settled outside.

The colour had returned to Sharon's cheeks, though she was very subdued, answering only monosyllabically when Sophia and Nikolaos spoke to her.

They drank their coffee beneath the star-spangled sky and listened to the rasp of the cicadas. Aleko and his father smoked cigars, sitting back contentedly in their padded cane chairs, and Sophia kept a concerned eye on the younger girl.

Kara alone was seething with anger and knew she could not return to the Hythes' without speaking to Aleko. 'I wonder,' she said, fixing what she hoped was a convincing smile to her lips, and looking directly at him, 'whether I could persuade you to show me around?'

'Of course he will,' agreed Sophia at once. 'I'd be disappointed if you didn't see the house. How about you, Sharon?'

Fortunately Sharon shook her head. 'I don't think I've got the energy.'

Dutifully Aleko rose to his feet, his eyes dark and enigmatic as they met Kara's. He knew exactly why she wanted to be alone with him.

'I know what you're thinking,' he said, the moment they were out of earshot, and before she could say anything herself, 'and I don't blame you for believing the worst of me. But it was best that your sister find out.'

'This way?' she demanded, coming to a standstill and facing him furiously. 'In front of strangers? It must be hell for her trying to pretend there's nothing wrong. You're a swine, Aleko; a cruel, cold-hearted, mean-minded brute, and I wish I were a man so that I could lay you flat on your back!'

'Take a punch at me now, if it will make you feel better,' he invited, looking amused.

'No, thank you.' She tossed her head haughtily. It would give her no satisfaction. Her blows would glance off his toughened body and she would end up with bruised knuckles. Her physical strength was pitiful compared to his.

'May I ask you a question?'

She looked at him guardedly.

'You knew about Katina. Why didn't you tell your sister?'

'Because,' she answered slowly and defensively, 'the time didn't seem right.'

He snorted angrily. 'Not right? When would it have been right? Once he had promised to marry her? When it was too late?'

Kara's blue eyes were more brilliant than they had ever been in her life. She was seething inside. 'It's true, that is what I hoped, but not for the reaons you think. I didn't want to worry my sister unnecessarily. If Petros truly loves Sharon, then what's the point in raking up past girlfriends?'

'If-Petros-truly-loves-Sharon?' he suggested dismissively, 'then I would be the first to agree with you, but it is not the case. She is blackmailing him, and rather than my parents find out—because he was on the verge of telling them the other day—I staged-managed this whole affair.' He gave a satisfied smile. 'I think now the romance will die a suitable death.'

Kara clenched her fists, filling her lungs with much-needed air. 'Is that what you really think?'

He looked smug. 'It's what I know.'

'You can't possibly know what's going on in Petros's mind,' she accused.

'No?' Black brows lifted. 'Petros has gone to Corfu to see which of the girls it is he really loves. If it was your sister do you think he would need to do such a thing? Sharon intrigues him, that's all. She's an attractive girl, I admit, and he is suffering a temporary infatuation. But as for marriage—pah!—it would not work. They are poles apart. She is the one who has done all the chasing, and I won't allow him to be trapped into a marriage that is wrong.'

'How dare you!' Kara defended her sister hotly. 'Sharon would never do such a thing. She truly loves your brother. There's no truth whatsoever in your accusation.'

'We've gone through all this,' Aleko said impatiently.

'And we'll go through it again, and again, until you realise that Sharon is sincere,' she declared, wondering how she could possibly ever have imagined that she was in love with this man. What an arrogant bastard he was! She hated him.

'Time will tell,' he said unconcernedly. 'The seeds of truth have been sown, and all we have to do now is wait for the outcome. If she really is pregnant, and Petros decides that it is Sharon he loves, then I will raise no more objections to their marriage.'

'Big of you,' scoffed Kara. 'When is he returning?'

He shrugged. 'I told him to take as much time as he needed to sort himself out.'

'You swine!' she snapped. 'What are you hoping to do, get me and Sharon off the island before he comes back?'

He grinned. 'That was the general idea. Don't you think we ought to carry on? Sophia will be sure to ask you all sorts of questions.'

Kara glared and followed him silently, gaining no pleasure from her conducted tour. She discovered that the house had indeed once belonged to royalty, some obscure Italian princess having had it built as her secret hideaway. But it had been in the Tranakas family for over a hundred years and it was hoped it would remain so for many more.

'And if neither of you have sons?'

His brows lifted fractionally. 'I intend to have a son.'

Such conceit! How could he possibly control something like that? 'How clever of you,' she commented drily. And yet it was just the sort of thing that would happen to Aleko. He was in total charge of his life. The only time things hadn't gone to plan was when the girl he loved had felt compelled to marry someone else.

They left the ballroom with its gilded ceiling and mirrored walls, and he took a key from his pocket and opened another door.

Kara frowned, and he answered her unspoken question. 'My own private wing.'

Her brows rose and apprehension quickened her heartbeats.

'You surely don't think I still live with my parents? At my age?' He sounded amused.

'I didn't give it a thought,' she said airily, 'but I don't think it's necessary for me to see in there.'

Aleko's eyes darkened. 'I appreciate the effort you made tonight, and I think it should be rewarded.'

Kara would have edged away had his hand not been on her back. She could feel each and every finger searing her naked skin, propelling her mercilessly forward. 'If I'd known what a heinous plot you'd devised I would never have come,' she grated through clenched teeth, 'and if you think you're going to take advantage of me you're very much mistaken. If you so much as lay another finger on me I shall scream!' She twisted angrily away.

The solid wooden door closed behind her. 'Scream all you like, *agape mou*. The walls are thick. No one will hear.'

His smile had never looked so sinister. Kara felt real fear. He was insane! 'But your parents will wonder why we're so long,' she protested.

'You are a beautiful girl. Do you not think they will guess? Have you no idea that is why Sophia suggested the tour? She thinks, because I invited you to meet them, that you are someone special. Sophia is anxious for me to find another girl to love.'

'Even an English girl?'

'As you heard my father say, her grandmother was English. They would both give their full approval.'

Kara swallowed hard. 'And yet you still think that I——' She could not finish. It was so ludicrous. She had never chased a man in her life. Aleko's wealth did not interest her. She had married for love the first time, mistaken though it was, and if—*if*—she ever got married again, it would be for love also. Only the next time she would be very very sure. She would get to know her chosen man as well as she knew herself. There would not be one facet of his character that she had not uncovered. And it certainly wouldn't be anyone like Aleko.

She changed her argument. 'In that case I can't see why they shouldn't approve of Petros marrying Sharon.'

By this time they had walked the length of a cool tiled corridor and he pushed open a door to a room that was totally different from the rest of the house.

It was comfortably furnished with a plump brown sofa and a couple of deep armchairs. A pair of Aleko's shoes littered the hearth and an open book lay face down beside them. There were no pictures on the plain white walls and no ornamentation on the ceiling. There was a pair of china horses on the rough-hewn stone fireplace and several souvenir ashtrays scattered around, but they were the only knick-knacks. Even the ashtrays were unused, his cigar stubs littering the grate instead. It was a room where one could relax. It was a lived-in room— and Kara loved it. She felt at home in it straight away.

'If Petros announced that he wanted to marry your sister, for the right reasons, they would not stop him,' he said, answering her almost forgotten question. 'But his reason is not the right one.'

'In your eyes only.' She wandered over to the window, but it was too dark to see anything except a canopy of stars—and Aleko's reflection behind her. She paused a moment, watching him. He came slowly and silently towards her. Was he hoping to take her by surprise? She turned quickly away and pretended an interest in one of the china horses.

'I am protecting my brother's interests, that is all,' he said. 'Do you like horses? I have several if you care to avail yourself of them. '

Kara turned scornful eyes on him. 'I thought I was supposed to be leaving the island?'

'I've decided that a few more days will make no difference. So long as Sharon goes when you do.' Again that hard inflection in his voice.

'I'm not making Sharon do what she doesn't want to do.'

'I think you might find she wants to leave after all.'

'Really?' she tossed scornfully. 'I imagine my sister will put her job first. She can't leave the Hythes until they find someone else. They're very satisfied with her. You'll be doing them a great disservice if you insist she goes.'

He moved closer towards her. 'I've not brought you here to discuss Sharon. So far as I'm concerned we've said all that needs to be said on that score. You looked radiant when you turned up here tonight, do you know that? Can I congratulate myself that I was responsible?' His hands fell on her shoulders and there was no way she could avoid looking at him.

'So what? I can't help being turned on by you, but I'm damned if I'm going to let you touch me again, after what you've just done. Get your hands of me!'

His lip curled derisively. 'That wasn't what you said when you were trying to worm your way into my life. Why should things be any different now? Since I've decided to let you stay on we might as well take advantage of the time you still have left. Except that now I know exactly where I stand.'

'Dammit, Aleko, when are you going to get it through your thick skull that I was playing no game?' She struggled furiously, but he simply laughed and slid his arms behind her back, pulling her hips hard against his.

'You're even more beautiful when you're angry.'

'And you'll be beautiful if I knee you where it hurts,' she threatened. 'Beautifully sore. Let go of me!'

'All in good time, *agape mou*, all in good time. I've wanted you all evening. You can't disappoint me now.'

CHAPTER EIGHT

ALEKO was in a very determined mood, and Kara felt fear as well as excitement. On no other occasion had he forced himself on her, and she wondered how far he would go if she continued to resist.

The trouble was that his body against hers set her adrenalin pumping and caused all sorts of unwanted sensations in the pit of her stomach, and she knew that it would be a simple matter for him to arouse her to the point of no return.

She felt his heart thud against her hand as he too was stirred by the contact. His eyes were half-closed, his mouth curved into a sensual smile, and the male scent of him drugged her senses.

'Relax, Kara.' His voice was deeper than usual, infinitely sexy. 'Admit that you want this as much as me.' He urged himself closer and there was no mistaking his arousal. He lowered his head and slowly and deliberately kissed every inch of her face. Each time his mouth touched her Kara felt her resistance getting lower and lower and lower, but she was still determined not to give in.

He was using unfair tactics. He knew how flimsy her defences were. A verbal battle she could handle, but her body had a mind of its own, and it liked the feel of Aleko, the pulsing strength of him, the expertise, the subtle methods of persuasion.

She made several futile attempts to pull away, but he was unmerciful. His hands edged up her back, exploring each contour and curve as if he were a blind man trying to commit her shape to memory.

When he reached her shoulders he slid aside the two thin crocheted straps, and ignoring her murmured protests bared her breasts to his hungry eyes. She knew the battle was almost over.

He slid an arm behind her back again, his thighs hard against hers. He claimed her mouth with his own, his tongue seeking the moist softness within, while his free hand shaped the pert thrust of one breast, his thumb brushing an already hardened nipple, his fingertips teasing and tormenting.

Kara's body moved helplessly against his, melting into him, all thoughts of resistance gone. And when his mouth moved down to supplement the exquisite pleasure his hand was giving, a moan escaped her arched throat. She moulded his head between her hands, holding him hard against her, her whole body ready for whatever he wanted to do.

But he was in no hurry, finishing one breast and then claiming the other, urging her to a deeper frenzy of emotion. What sweet torture it was! When he lifted his head, his lips soft and warm from her, his eyes were glazed, and when he kissed her mouth again Kara released every last atom of pride, responding wantonly, her hunger primitive, her whole body aching desperately for fulfilment.

'How do you feel now, sweet Kara?' he murmured huskily.

'I want you, Aleko,' she breathed, looking straight into the hot blackness of his eyes. 'God forgive me, I can't help myself. You affect me like no other man ever has.'

'Not even your husband?' he gruffed.

'Not even Greg.' The painful admission was forced from her.

In actual fact what she had experienced with Greg was pitiful compared to the depth of hunger Aleko was able to arouse. She ought not to have let it happen. Hadn't she promised herself she would never get involved with another man unless she knew beyond any shadow of doubt that he truly loved her? What had happened to that promise? Why had she let Aleko get so close?

But it was too late for self-recrimination. She was here, in Aleko's arms, wanting him, needing him desperately, unable to quell the aching hunger inside her.

'That's a surprising admission,' he said, his eyes hardening fractionally. 'What's happened, has your plan backfired?'

Her eyes snapped and she strove to free herself, but with a harsh laugh he clamped his lips on hers. 'Poor little Kara,' he mouthed cruelly. 'This is going to be a more pleasurable experience than I expected. It's my turn now to have the upper hand.'

His lips bruised hers suddenly, his hands urgently chasing over her body. The button on her skirt came undone at a touch, the zip slid down with indecent haste, and within seconds the garment was around her ankles. Her camisole top followed and then her white lacy briefs.

Kara's first instinct when she stood naked before him was to cover herself with her hands. But she had shown no shyness on the occasion she had slept in his bed, so why now?

Her chin lifted proudly and she made herself look him in the eye. 'Now what?'

'You're going to beg me to make love to you.'

She closed her eyes. How easily he could make her do

that! She was putty in his hands, and he knew it, and it was giving him a great deal of pleasure.

The rustle of his clothes made her look at him sharply. He was disrobing too. Kara ran the tip of her tongue across her lips and swallowed a sudden constricting lump in her throat. Her mouth was so dry.

'Have you nothing to say?'

She shook her head.

His eyes ran the whole length of her body, lingering over-long on her aching breasts, probing intimately the feminine heart of her. Her pulses quickened, her whole body throbbing with need and desire.

If he wanted her why didn't he take her? She had not the strength to resist. Surely he knew that? Why did he subject her to this disturbing scrutiny which was affecting her senses as much as if he were physically making contact?

'Touch me, Kara.'

As though she were a robot controlled by a computer, Kara responded to the tone of his voice, lifting her hands and placing them on his shoulders.

'Like this, here.' He took her hands and put them on his chest, guiding her over the hard contours of his body. She fought shy of actually touching him intimately, but she put her arms behind his back and pulled him close against her.

His hair-roughened skin tormented her breasts and accelerated her heartbeats, and within seconds she was gyrating against him, feeling his pulsing response and wanting him more urgently than ever.

'That's better.' His voice was gruff in her ear, but he still made her do all the work, not touching her until her movements grew more demanding.

Then suddenly his mouth was hungry on hers and he

swung her up into his arms as though she were no heavier than a sack full of feathers.

The sofa was long and soft and accommodated them both easily. His hands explored and incited until Kara was crying out for fulfilment, her fingers biting deep into his shoulders, her mouth and tongue feeding on the masculine taste of his skin.

'Now, Kara? Now?' he demanded.

She nodded, hardly conscious of what she was doing.

'You want me to make love to you?'

Again she inclined her head.

'Then say it. Say it, Kara. Say it now.'

The throbbing tone of his voice woke some responsive chord and she remembered. Hell, no, she wouldn't beg him; she would die of frustration first. 'If you want me,' she whispered, 'you take me, but I'll never ask. Never!'

She kept her eyes closed, but she could guess at the hardening of his face, the widening of his nostrils, the muscles jerking in his jaw. This wasn't what he wanted at all.

'Then it looks as if we've reached stalemate,' he said hardly. 'Are you sure, Kara? Are you sure you're not hurting yourself to spite me?' He teased the engorged nipples of her breasts, nipping them between his teeth, setting off a whole new series of aches and needs and desires.

Kara did not know how much longer she could last without demanding that he finish what he had started. She swallowed and moistened her dry mouth. 'Damn you, Aleko! I'm sure.'

His lips curled. 'Then it's your loss, not mine.' With effortless ease he lifted himself off her. For a moment he stood looking down with fathomless eyes, not a hint at all on his face that her rejection meant anything to him. Then he calmly proceeded to get dressed, looking across at her from time to time, his eyes glinting now with amusement.

God, what a swine he was! It really had meant nothing to him. He was entirely capable of turning his feelings on and off at will.

When he had finished dressing he picked up her clothes and tossed them on to the sofa beside her. 'If you'd like to use the bathroom, it's through there.' He crossed to a cabinet and began to pour himself a Scotch, and Kara made sure that when he turned round she had gone.

She took a quick shower, conscious of the fact that it was his soap she was using to try and rid herself of the feel of him, his towel to dry her mistreated body, his comb to tidy her tangled hair. When she had finished she felt no better, and when she rejoined him she could not look him in the eye.

She stood by the door waiting for them to leave and he came and stood beside her, lifting her chin, compelling her to look at him. 'My parents will ask questions if you go back looking like that. Forget all the names you'd like to call me. Remember only the good times we've had together. And I'll be quite willing to—lend you the services of my body before you go back to England—if you feel the need.'

Kara lifted her hand to slap the tormenting smile off his face, but he caught her wrist easily, his jaw firming as he held it up in front of her face. 'Don't do that,' he grated, all mockery gone, anger glinting in his eyes.

'Then don't make fun of me,' she thrust. 'I've had as much of you as I can stomach. Don't flatter yourself that

I'll ever need you again!'

His mood changed once more with lightning speed. He grinned. 'The human body is a fickle thing, I should not be too sure.'

'I'll make sure,' she spat. 'Can we please go?'

With exaggerated politeness he opened the door and they walked together down the silent corridor. Kara breathed a sigh of relief when they reached the main part of the house and the door to his wing was safely locked.

'Don't forget to look as though you've had a good time,' he threatened softly just before they reached the others. He caught her hand and spun her to look at him, his smile gentle, with no hint at all of the hard character beneath. He brushed back a stray strand of hair and his fingers lingered on her cheek. 'I meant it when I said you were beautiful.'

Kara's grimace was wry, but she could not help feeling flattered, and when they joined his parents and Sharon there was no hint on her face of the battle she had just fought.

'Your home's beautiful,' she said feelingly to Sophia and Nikolaos, 'just as I thought it would be. Thank you so much for letting me see it.' She turned her attention to her sister. 'How are you, Sharon? Would you like to go home?'

Sharon nodded.

'Would you mind very much?' Kara enquired of her hosts.

'Not at all,' said Sophia understandingly, 'but you must promise to come again before you go back to England. I've so enjoyed having you both.'

Kara glanced at Aleko, whose face was impassive. 'It's very kind of you,' she answered quietly, 'but I'm not sure whether I'll have the time. There's still so much I want to do.'

Aleko knew she was lying and she caught the smile lifting his lips. 'I'll see what I can do to persuade her,' he said.

Sophia looked satisfied. 'You do that, Aleko. It's been such a pleasant evening. I hope you'll feel better soon, Sharon, and the invitation includes you too, of course.'

'Thank you,' murmured Sharon.

'Nikolaos,' continued the older woman, 'you'd better tell Spiros to bring the car round.'

Kara half expected Aleko to say that he would drive them home, but he simply stood there with a half-smile on his lips, his hands pushed into his trouser pockets. He looked entirely relaxed and satisfied, and it would have given her much pleasure to wipe the smile off his face.

All the way home Sharon was silent, but the moment they stepped out of the car she turned furiously on Kara. 'Did you know Petros wouldn't be there?' she demanded.

Kara could not lie. 'Aleko did suggest he might not be.'

'Then why on earth did you keep it to yourself?' her sister demanded. 'I wouldn't have gone if I'd known. Did he say where Petros was?'

Kara shook her head.

Sharon clearly did not believe her. 'But you knew about Katina?' she questioned furiously. 'I could see by your face it wasn't news to you. Why didn't you tell me?'

Kara heaved a sigh. 'Keep your voice down, Sharon, unless you want the Hythes to come out and see what's going on.'

Her sister tossed her head impatiently and began to

move away from the house. 'You did know?' she insisted.

Kara nodded reluctantly. 'But I thought it best to say nothing.'

'You wanted me to make a fool of myself?'

'No, not that,' protested Kara. 'I hoped Katina might prove to be a has-been. I didn't want to worry you unnecessarily.'

'She doesn't sound very much like a has-been to me,' retorted Sharon vehemently. 'Childhood sweethearts, his father said. Any day now they're expecting wedding bells. Oh, Kara, what am I going to do?'

The girl broke down in sudden tears, and Kara gathered her into her arms, holding her close until the sobs abated. 'You can do nothing until Petros gets back. Aleko says he's gone to check on his feelings for Katina. He did love her—until you turned up. Now he's confused and needs to make sure before finally committing himself.'

Sharon's wails began all over again. 'So you knew all along? Why did you lie? Oh, God, I wish I were dead! I wish Petros hadn't saved me the other day!'

Kara felt alarmed by the fierceness of her sister's outburst. 'I didn't know in the beginning,' she said gently. 'Aleko told me when he showed me over the house. Apparently it was Aleko's idea that Petros go and see Katina.'

'I might have known!' Sharon's head jerked, her eyes feverishly bright. 'He still thinks I'm lying just so that Petros will marry me. Oh, I wish Petros had told me about Katina. I wish someone had told me. Why didn't he, Kara? Why? He swore he loved me, and I believed him.'

Kara swallowed hard. 'Until he returns I think you

should try and look on the bright side. He said he loved you, didn't he? But it's only fair on Katina that he tells her the truth.'

She mentally crossed her fingers. Her own experience with men did not give her much hope. Damn Greg, and damn Aleko. They made her suspicious of every single male. How could she convince Sharon, feeling as she did?

'If Petros—decides he loves Katina—better than me, I shall come home with you, Kara.'

'And let the Hythes down? I shouldn't make too hasty a decision. There's the baby to think of too. I have a feeling it might influence Petros in your favour.'

'I don't want him to marry me just for the baby's sake,' cried Sharon.

Kara held her close. 'I know. Let's go in. You look as though you're ready to drop on your feet.'

Fortunately Rosemary and Geoff were nowhere in sight, so they were able to go up to Sharon's room without questions being asked.

'Would you like me to stay with you for a while?' asked Kara, not happy about her sister. Sharon's face had no trace of colour, her eyes red-rimmed, her limbs trembling so much she could hardly stand.

'I'm all right,' murmured Sharon.

'You don't look it. Can I get you a brandy or something?'

'Oh, stop fussing!' she cried. 'Just leave me alone!' Fresh tears raced down her cheeks and she threw herself face downwards on the bed.

Kara laid her hand on Sharon's heaving shoulders. 'Sharon, please, don't upset yourself any more. Everything will work out all right, I'm sure.'

'Don't humour me,' snapped Sharon, 'Just go away. I

don't want to talk to you any more. You haven't helped me, not one little bit. '

Kara pulled a wry face and reluctantly left the room. There was nothing more she could do.

She stood at the window and looked in the direction of the Tranakas villa. Its black shape was barely visible against the night sky. There was one pinpoint of light from a window, which even as she watched was extinguished. Was it Aleko? she wondered. Was his wing visible from here?

She despised herself for the way she had reacted earlier and wished with all her heart that she could turn the clock back. She could still feel his hands and his mouth on her and turning away from the window in disgust she undressed and got into bed. It had been an evening to remember.

The next morning Rosemary asked Kara whether she would mind looking after Amanda and Damien. 'Sharon's not feeling too good. She says not to worry, but actually I don't think she's looked well for some time.'

'I'm sure it can't be much,' Kara said quickly. 'She was perfectly all right last night.' It was not her place to tell Rosemary Hythe about Sharon's condition, especially at this early stage. 'I'll go up to her in a minute. And of course I'll look after the twins—it will be a pleasure. Where are they now?'

'Playing in their room,' Rosemary told her, looking relieved. 'I've told them they must be very quiet and very good. Unfortunately I have to work full-time for a couple of weeks—Aleko's secretary's away on holiday and he's asked me if I'll take over.' She smiled her pleasure. 'You can't imagine what a relief it is to have you here. I know it's your holiday and I wouldn't ask if it wasn't necessary, but I should hate to let him down.'

Rosemary never bothered to hide her admiration of Aleko. What would she say, Kara wondered, if she knew how he was treating her and Sharon? He wasn't quite the saint she supposed.

'And you must tell me some time about last night,' Rosemary went on. 'I'm sure you had a marvellous time. I'm sorry I can't stop now, but I'm late already.'

Kara did not expect to find anything really wrong with Sharon. Her sister had probably spent the night crying and was too embarrassed to show her face. And this was exactly what she found. Sharon's eyes were puffed up, her skin blotchy, and she looked thoroughly miserable.

'Sharon,' accused Kara sharply, 'you can't lie here all day feeling sorry for yourself. I suggest you get up and wash your face and snap out of it. You don't even know for sure what Petros is going to do. At least give him the benefit of the doubt.'

Her sister eyed her resentfully. 'It's not that. I don't feel well, I really don't.'

'Do you feel sick?' asked Kara, drawing a perfectly natural conclusion.

But Sharon shook her head. 'I ache all over, and I'm too weak to even get out of bed.'

Kara's matter-of-factness turned to concern. 'I'd better arrange for a doctor to come over.'

'No, please don't.'

'Why?' Kara looked at her sister sharply. 'Because of the baby?'

Sharon nodded. 'I don't want the Hythes to know yet. If—if Petros—if he doesn't want me any more—then I shall go home, and they need never know.'

'They'll be even less pleased if you leave them in the lurch.'

'They'll find someone,' shrugged Sharon. 'There's a girl in the village who would be delighted to look after them. She joins us sometimes when we go to the beach. The twins adore her.'

She had all the answers, decided Kara. 'And meantime, what are we going to do about you? Have you any idea at all what can be wrong?'

Sharon grimaced. 'Actually I think I've caught the twins' virus—their symptoms were exactly the same. Two or three days in bed and I'll be as right as rain.'

'I hope you can convince Rosemary of that,' said Kara. 'She's very worried. She's working full-time at the moment, did you know?'

'Oh, no!' groaned Sharon. 'What's happening about Amanda and Damien?'

'She's asked me to look after them.'

'But you can't spend your last days like that.'

Kara shrugged. 'I don't think Rosemary thought you'd be ill for more than a day.'

'She'll have to take time off,' said Sharon firmly.

Kara pulled a face. 'Normally I'm sure she would, but she's filling in for someone who's on holiday. You've chosen a bad time to be ill, Sharon.'

Her attempt at humour failed to cheer her sister. 'This is the last thing I want on top of everything else,' Sharon groaned. 'At least when I'm working I don't have time to worry about Petros and the baby. Now I shall have nothing to do but lie and think.'

'I'll bring the twins in to cheer you up.'

Sharon groaned. 'No, thanks. Get me some aspirin and a glass of fruit juice and then leave me alone. My head's splitting!'

Amanda and Damien were as good as gold all day long, tiptoeing about the house, speaking only in whispers, and even when Kara took them to the pool they kept their voices unusually low.

When Rosemary came home they told her how good they had been, and she congratulated them and played with them, then gave them their supper and put them to bed.

'I felt so guilty about leaving you to look after them,' she said to Kara later, 'that I told Aleko about Sharon and said my duty lay at home.' She smiled ruefully. 'So the rest of your holiday is your own.'

'You didn't have to do that,' protested Kara, even though secretly she was relieved. She had not relished the thought of spending her last few days baby-sitting.

'Apparently it's a good job I did,' added Rosemary. 'Sharon seems to think she's caught the twins' virus, in which case it will be a day or two before she's well enough to take over again.'

That night Aleko phoned Kara. Rosemary smiled knowingly as she handed over the receiver, then tactfully left the room.

Still the incurable romantic, thought Kara, holding the phone as though it were a live bomb about to explode. 'Hello, Aleko,' she said, her tone wary, unable to imagine why he should be phoning her, unless it was to gloat over his success the night before. Why the hell had she responded? Why couldn't she be strong?

'Kara, I have a proposition to put to you.'

Her eyes widened. What sort of a proposition? The mind boggled. But she lifted her chin determinedly. 'Whatever it is, I'm not interested.'

'I thought you might say that.' She could tell by his tone that he was smiling. 'I'm coming to pick you up in fifteen minutes. We'll discuss it over a meal.'

'You'll be lucky,' retorted Kara. 'You can't make me——' But she was talking to thin air. The line had already gone dead.

The nerve of the man! One minute he was trying to get rid of her, the next he was—what? She wished she knew. Did he intend proposing that they make the most of her last days here?

Or was it something more devious than that? Had he dreamt up some heinous plot to hurt her because he was still not convinced about her sincerity? She compressed her lips. Whatever, she would be on her guard. There would certainly be no repetition of last night. She had given herself to him for the last time.

His car drew up outside the Hythes' house in less than fifteen minutes. 'He's certainly keen!' smiled Rosemary, Kara having told her that she was going out with Aleko.

'I doubt if we'll be long,' she said shortly, ignoring the questioning look Rosemary gave her.

She opened the door just as he was about to ring the bell. He smiled widely. 'You're ready—good. I don't like to be kept waiting.'

Contrarily Kara wished she hadn't been so prompt. 'I don't see why we have to go out at all,' she spat. 'Couldn't you have said what you wanted on the phone?'

He wore denims and a T-shirt and looked nothing like the man she had left last night. He was no less sexy, though, in fact quite the opposite. The tight jeans accentuated and revealed his masculinity, and her heart annoyingly skipped a few beats.

'I could have done,' he said, 'but I know what your answer would have been.'

'Most probably no,' she spat. 'I don't really want

anything to do with any suggestion of yours. It's sure to be designed to hurt me in the end.'

'You're wrong,' he said, 'entirely wrong. This time I'm asking you a favour.'

She frowned.

'Jump in,' he urged. 'We'll discuss it on the way.'

His car was too intimate for comfort, especially after the fool she had made of herself last night. The few inches between them were not enough to dispel her awareness of him. She sat as far away as she possibly could. A favour? She could not imagine Aleko asking favours of anyone.

For the first few minutes they drove in silence, heading up into the mountains. It was dusk and he took the hairpin bends perilously close, and Kara was glad he did not try to engage her in conversation.

And then the road straightened out and he glanced at her and smiled, and Kara held her breath. 'I realise this might come as something of a surprise,' he said, 'but I want to ask whether you'll consider working for me.'

A surprise? It was a complete shock. 'Why?' she demanded. 'What's the ulterior motive?'

'No motive,' he shrugged. 'My secretary's on holiday, and——'

'You want me to do the job you asked Rosemary to do?' she enquired abruptly.

'That's right. She said Sharon's ill?' His brows rose, and it was not difficult to guess what interpretation he had put on that. 'And Rosemary made so many mistakes yesterday, presumably her conscience bothering her because she'd had to ask you to look after the children, that I'm better off without her.'

'If it's a choice between looking after the twins, or working for you, then I know which I shall choose,' she commented bitterly. 'What are you trying to do, make sure my last few days here are hell?'

'Is your opinion of me so low?' he questioned harshly.

'It's rock bottom,' she crisped, 'as yours is of me.'

His mouth firmed. 'I'm serious, Kara. Will you do the work?'

She shook her head firmly. 'No.'

'Why? I'm not asking you do it for nothing.'

'I wouldn't do it for nothing,' she snapped, 'but at least if I'm looking after the twins I can still sunbathe or explore or swim, or do whatever takes my fancy. Sitting in an office is no different from what I do back at home. Are there no agencies you can apply to?'

'On the mainland, yes,' he snarled, 'but it would take time and I need someone straight away. My work cannot wait. We are very short-staffed as it is, and I was relying on Rosemary. Your sister's certainly chosen an inopportune moment to fall ill!'

'You say that as though you think she'd done it deliberately!' crisped Kara.

His lips firmed. 'I do not wish to get into an argument about your sister, even though it's a coincidence—this illness of hers. I take it she was not happy about the news she received last night?'

'What do you think?' she spat. 'But actually, she's caught a virus. It's as simple as that.' And if he went on any more about Sharon she would swipe him one.

'I see.' He paused, then said, 'But back to my offer. I shall pay you well, naturally, and I see no reason why you should not add the number of days you work on to the end of your holiday.'

'Oh, yes,' retorted Kara, 'I'm sure my boss would love that. I'm due back at my desk on Monday morning.'

'I'll get in touch with him,' said Aleko imperiously.

'Give me his name and telephone number.'

'My answer is still no,' she thrust. 'And I have no wish to discuss it further.'

'You leave me no choice.' Gone was the persuasive smile, the softness in his dark eyes. His jaw firmed ruthlessly and when he looked at her again his face was a mask of anger.

Kara felt a quiver of alarm at the implied threat, but she lifted her chin and eyed him bravely. 'No choice, Mr Tranakas? I thought this was a free world we lived in? The choice is mine, as well you know, and if I choose not to work for you there's nothing at all you can do about it.'

'No?' An eyebrow quirked. 'Let me put it this way. If you continue to refuse I shall personally escort you and your sister off this island first thing tomorrow morning. And I shall make sure she never sees or hears from Petros again.'

'Even if she's carrying his child?' cried Kara, unable to believe that he could be so cruel.

'If, Kara? I thought she was sure?'

Kara cursed her slip. 'Well, she is—I mean, as sure as she can be until she has a pregnancy test.'

'Which she should have had done before saying anything,' he condemned icily. 'I mean what I say, Kara. Baby or no baby, you both go.'

'You bastard!' She could not believe that he meant it. He had said earlier that if her sister were really pregnant he would not object to them marrying. He was bluffing. Wasn't he? But could she afford to take the risk?

She hated seeing Sharon upset. Last night, when her sister heard about Katina, she had almost broken her heart. If they were parted, without her being given the opportunity to speak to Petros again, it would finish her altogether. She might even go so far as to take her own life. Kara was not altogether sure that the incident at sea had been an accident; Sharon was in a very emotional state at that moment.

'Well, Kara, I am waiting.'

Her eyes met his in a blaze of anger. 'Damn you, Aleko!'

'Does that mean you agree?' he enquired smoothly.

'As you said, I have no choice,' she gritted. 'But don't expect me to be friendly. Because I wish you were in hell!'

CHAPTER NINE

ALEKO was in a jubilant mood for the rest of the evening. Kara had expected and indeed wanted him to take her back, but instead they had ended up at the same little taverna as before.

'*Stin iyia sas*,' he said. 'Cheers,' raising his glass.

Their eyes met and she looked daggers at him before turning quickly away. He was so damned smug and cheerful she could have quite happily flung her wine in his face.

There was silence all about them, and not a breath of wind. Far below lay the rugged coastline, a jagged edge between the turquoise sea and the green mantle of vines that cloaked the mountain.

She would miss all this when she went back to England. The island held plenty of bad memories, but there were good ones too—and all connected with this man.

When she brought her attention back to the table Aleko was watching her, his eyes narrowed, his arm resting across the back of her chair. 'How long is this cold-shoulder treatment going to last, Kara?'

'Until I leave the island,' she glared. 'It's not going to be fun, having me work for you, I'll tell you that now.'

His eyes narrowed. 'It is not intended to be—fun. There is too much to do. But in your leisure time, surely you do not intend keeping up this—ridiculous charade?'

She held his gaze boldly. 'You think we should still make love—when we get the chance? You see no reason why we shouldn't enjoy each other's bodies? God, Aleko, you make me sick! Is that all you ever think about?'

'When you're around, yes,' he admitted, a slow smile curving his lips.

'Then it will be my pleasure to see you suffer,' she spat savagely. 'For if you so much as lay a finger on me I shall cry rape—no matter where we are.'

His brows lifted. 'Do you know, Kara, I believe you mean that.'

'If you have any doubts then try me,' she challenged.

'Oh, I will,' he said, 'make no mistake about that. But not here, not yet.'

Some of Kara's bravado faded. He intended waiting until they were out of earshot—like on the way home! And there was not a darn thing she could do about it. But by God, she would put up a fight! She would never melt into his arms again.

It was a relief when Yanni appeared with the lobster Aleko had ordered. 'You enjoy this, I hope?' he said, placing the dish in front of them.

'Anything you cook, Yanni, is superb,' smiled Aleko.

And it was delicious. Kara could not remember tasting anything so succulent in a long time. Despite the fact that she had not felt hungry she now picked eagerly at the lobster and the salad, and drank more wine, and gradually felt some of the tension go out of her.

It grew dark, and candles were lit on the tables and Greek music filled the air. Yanni himself donned a red shirt and danced for them, and by the end of the evening Kara had almost forgotten the way Aleko had black-mailed her.

On the drive home she lay back in her seat and closed her eyes, feeling pleasantly lightheaded. Aleko had kept refilling her glass and she had drunk a lot more than she intended. He sang softly in Greek, his deep voice soothing, and the next thing Kara knew he was waking her outside the Hythes' villa.

To her embarrassment she found her head on his shoulder. With a cry she sat bolt upright, her eyes fixed widely on him. 'It's all right,' he said, with an amused smile. 'I've not touched you. I prefer my partner awake when I'm making love.'

Kara swore beneath her breath and struggled from the car. The fresh night air felt good and she stood for a moment inhaling deeply. 'You don't get many nights like this in England,' said Aleko, appearing silently at her side.

'And I don't need you to see me into the house,' she returned sharply.

But he ignored her protest. 'I will collect you in the morning at eight-thirty sharp,' he announced as she opened the door.

Kara glanced at him sharply. 'Why, don't you trust me? I can easily get a lift with Geoff.'

He looked at her for several long seconds before shrugging his broad shoulders. 'As you wish. *Kalinikta*, Kara. Do not be late.'

Resisting the urge to kick his shins, Kara closed the door and tiptoed upstairs, popping her head round Sharon's door, pleased to see that her sister was asleep and looked more peaceful than she had earlier in the day.

The next morning Kara was woken out of a jumbled dream by her alarm. She felt worried and uneasy. She had almost drowned in the sea because she was drunk when she went swimming, Greg was in bed with another woman, none of her clothes would fit, she had lost her wedding ring and couldn't find it anywhere. It was a mad illogical dream and she felt completely disorientated.

She dragged on a towelling robe and stumbled through to the bathroom, standing beneath the shower for at least ten minutes. She felt more alive but still apprehensive, and knew it was because she was beginning work for Aleko today. It was a daunting thought.

Sharon was still in bed, feeling too weak as yet to get up, and when she heard Kara's news she looked shocked. 'How could you? I thought you hated the sight of him?'

'I did. I still do—sometimes.' Kara did not dare tell her sister that Aleko had blackmailed her.

'I think you're making a big mistake,' said Sharon, and then changed the subject completely. 'Has Petros come back?'

Kara shook her head. 'I don't think so.'

Sharon sighed and turned away. 'You'd better go,' she mumbled, her voice thick. 'His lordship won't like it if you keep him waiting.'

Kara closed her eyes, groaning inwardly. How difficult it all was! 'I'm sure everything will turn out fine. You wait and see.'

'Aleko's really got you where he wants you, hasn't he?' claimed Sharon, turning her head swiftly.

Kara was shocked to see the anger in her sister's eyes. 'What do you mean?'

'You don't care what he's doing to me, so long as you're having a good time.'

'That's not true,' protested Kara at once, a lump rising in her throat. 'Aleko didn't force Petros to go and see Katina—he only suggested it.'

'In such a way that Petros couldn't refuse,' spat Sharon. 'And the fact that he's not come straight back tells me what I need to know. It's all over between us.'

'You're being melodramatic because you're not feeling well,' said Kara sympathetically. 'I'm sorry, but I can't stand here arguing now. We'll talk about it tonight. Who knows, Petros might have returned by then.' She backed sorrowfully out of the room, hating the look of despair on her sister's face, wishing there was something she could do about it.

Her day was hell. Aleko was brusque, authoritative, and expected so much of her it was unbelievable. She wondered whether any work had been done at all on this new project.

There were lists to be drawn up and fed into the computer of all the main wholesalers in the UK, lists of all his wines. There were letters of introduction to be drafted and approved. More lists of the top chains of hotels and restaurants where he hoped to supply his wines direct. Confirmation of his attendance at a wine festival in Birmingham, a catalogue of the wines he would be exhibiting.

There was enough work to keep her going for weeks, not the few days she had expected, and at the end of the day she was both angry and exhausted. Even the fact that Aleko had been called away to Athens did not improve her temper.

Geoff grinned unconcernedly when she complained. 'Aleko has a reputation for being a hard taskmaster, but he's lavish in his praise when work is well done,' he assured her. 'He's fair, if nothing else, is Aleko Tranakas. You'll soon get used to him.'

Fair? Aleko? Who was he kidding? Had he any idea at all of the duress she was under? What would he say if she told him that Aleko had forced her into the job? He would laugh, probably. He would never believe her.

Even her boss in England had been remarkably agreeable when Aleko rang to say that she was extending her holiday. Whether it was the case of wines he had been promised, or whether Aleko's charm had worked wonders over the telephone, she did not know, but Mr Coombes said she was not to worry and he was glad she was able to help Mr Tranakas out. Help him out indeed! He was obviously under the illusion that she had volunteered.

The next three days followed a similar pattern, and by the time she got home each evening Kara was exhausted, though to be truthful she found it exciting to be in at the beginning of a new venture.

Sharon continued to worry her. Her sister did not seem to be getting any better. She barely ate and was snappy with everyone, even the twins, whom she normally adored. It was no longer the virus, Kara felt sure, Sharon was breaking her heart over Petros.

'You can't go on like this,' she said one night, when Sharon seemed even more withdrawn than usual. 'You're not being fair on Rosemary. She's taken time off on your account—and she was very much looking forward to working for Aleko. What do you think she'll say if she discovers you're not really ill, that all you're doing is eating your heart out for a man who——'

'Who doesn't want me any longer,' burst out Sharon. 'Go on, say it. Oh, hell, why did I let it happen? I've made a real fool of myself, haven't I? I can't stay here any longer, Kara, I can't. I'm sorry for the Hythes, but it would kill me to stay now. What if I bumped into Petros? What would I say? What would I do? He's made it perfectly clear that it's all over, that it's Katina he prefers. God, I wish I were dead!'

'Sharon, please.' Kara cringed inwardly at this

further reference to taking her own life. 'Don't distress yourself.'

She sat on the edge of the bed and hugged her sister, who had grown into such a pale shadow of her former self. There were huge purple smudges beneath her eyes and no colour at all in her face. Her normally shiny bouncing hair lay lank and dull on the pillow. Her effervescence had completely disappeared, and Kara was more deeply disturbed than she would admit. It was time something was done about it. She could not allow Sharon to go on like this.

'You don't understand,' wailed Sharon. 'Go away and leave me alone!'

Kara understood only too well. Hadn't her world been smashed into a million pieces when she discovered what Greg had been up to behind her back? Oh, she understood, much better than Sharon could ever guess. But time alone would be her sister's healer, and even then she would never be able to permanently erase her memories. For one thing, she would have Petros's baby, and what could be more permanent than that? How many times had she, Kara, thanked her lucky stars that she had no such reminder of Greg?

'You're making a grave mistake, letting him upset you like this,' she said gently. 'Come on, Sharon, get yourself up and take a shower, then we'll go and sit outside. It's gone cooler. It's lovely and fresh, almost like England.'

But Sharon fought off her arms and her good intentions. 'I'm not listening to you, Kara—just go away and leave me alone. When I move out of this bed it will be to catch a plane home. If you want to do me a favour, then just book my ticket.'

Kara shook her head, sighing, and aching inside.

Perhaps, after all, returning to England was the best thing her sister could do. It really did look as though Petros had no intention of returning. And her mother would stand no nonsense, she would soon chivvy some sense into Sharon.

It came as a shock to Kara when Petros appeared in her office the next morning. She had lain awake half the night worrying about her sister, and now here was the man responsible for her deteriorating condition.

He looked distraught. 'Tell me about Sharon, she is all right?'

Kara eyed him hardly, seeing the fear in his eyes, the lines of strain on his face, but was not moved by it. 'Not exactly.'

'I wish you had got in touch with me. I would straight away have come back. I did not know she was ill.' He seemed to be putting the blame on her.

'My sister wants more than your sympathy,' she reproved coldly.

'Yesterday I tried to telephone Sharon, but she would not speak to me,' he claimed worriedly. 'Please tell me what is wrong. Is it the baby?' He was wringing his hands in despair, his dark eyes deeply disturbed.

'No,' said Kara, more softly this time, and surprised to hear he had attempted to get in touch with her sister. 'The baby has nothing to do with it.'

'Then what?' he frowned.

'Initially she had a virus infection, but now——' She paused and eyed him accusingly. 'I think she's suffering from a broken heart, and who can blame her? You go away without so much as a word!' Her voice rose sharply. 'I know it was Aleko's doing, but even so you could have given Sharon some sort of explanation—even if it wasn't the whole truth.'

'I am sorry,' he said, and then a slow smile spread across his face. 'I am happy that Sharon is all right, though. I wanted to tell her about me and Katina. I——'

Himself and Katina? Petros and Katina. The two linked names shot an arrow of alarm through Kara and her eyes narrowed. He did not have to tell her—she knew what he was going to say—it was written all over his face. He looked ecstatic. Poor Sharon, her worst fears were about to be realised.

'I have had some long talks with her,' he was saying, 'and I——'

'Petros! I have found you at last.' Aleko's stern voice cut Petros short. 'Do you not care that you have much work to do? You can talk to Kara later—if it is that important.' He glared at Kara as though it was her fault for keeping the younger man talking. 'And I'm sure you also are far too busy to indulge in idle conversation.'

'It wasn't exactly idle——' she began, but he stopped her with an imperative lift of one hand.

'Whatever you were discussing this is neither the time nor the place. You are both paid to work, not chatter.'

With a resentful glance Petros slid out of the room. Kara glared angrily. 'Petros was here for no more than a minute. You had no right to interrupt.'

'Silence!' he snarled. 'I want this typed before lunch.' He threw a piece of paper on the desk in front of her and then strode back towards the door, turning abruptly at the last minute.

'By the way, you are invited once more to the villa for dinner tonight.'

Her fine brows rose.

'Sophia's idea this time, not mine.' Aleko answered

her unspoken question.

'Is Sharon invited too?' she demanded coolly.

'Naturally.'

But Kara knew Sharon would not go, and she wished she could find some excuse to get out of it herself. The trouble was she genuinely liked Sophia and did not want to disappoint her.

To her astonishment Sharon was sitting by the pool when she got home, watching Rosemary and the twins swimming. 'What a wonderful surprise!' Kara slid into a chair beside the younger girl. 'I'm glad you're feeling better.'

'I'm not,' snapped Sharon, her blue eyes angry. But she had washed her hair and despite her negative statement looked a thousand times fitter than she had the night before.

'You never said Petros had phoned you yesterday. Why wouldn't you speak to him?'

Sharon clamped her lips. 'What was there to say? He's made the whole position perfectly clear. It doesn't take that long to make your mind up about someone.'

'He came to see me this morning. He was very—concerned about you.'

'I bet he was!' Sharon hunched her shoulders. 'Concerned enough to stay away for nearly a week. I've told Rosemary I'm leaving.'

Kara groaned inwardly. So this really was the end. 'Did you tell her why?' she asked.

Sharon shook her head.

'Don't you think you should?'

'It's none of her business,' cried Sharon sharply, 'just as it's none of yours. Why won't you leave me alone?'

Kara heaved a sigh. Sharon was growing more and more unreasonable. Perhaps it was as well she wanted to go home. 'We've been invited to the Tranakas' for dinner tonight,' she said softly.

Sharon swung about, her eyes glittering with pain and anger and defeat. 'No, thank you very much. I don't want to see Petros. I'm sick of him up to here.' She lifted her hand to her chin. 'Just tell him to stay out of my life.'

'That might not be so easy,' said Kara softly. 'He's the baby's father. '

'He's forfeited all rights, by going back to Katina. The baby's mind—mine, mine, mine!' The girl's voice rose shrilly, and Rosemary looked across.

Kara tried to smile reassuringly, and Sharon heaved herself to her feet. 'I'm going back to my room.'

When Kara followed she found Sharon had locked the door, and she resigned herself to the fact that her sister would not speak to her again today.

She lay on her bed for a while, listening to the children squealing outside, then she helped Rosemary get them ready for bed.

'I'm sorry Sharon's decided to leave,' Kara said. 'I hope it won't inconvenience you too much.'

Rosemary lifted her shoulders in a faint shrug. 'I've sensed for some time that she hasn't been happy. I wasn't altogether surprised. I expect she's missing her family and friends.'

Kara murmured something non-committal. 'Do you think you'll be able to find someone to replace her?' she asked.

'If I don't then I'll look after them myself,' smiled Rosemary. 'Isn't it what all good mothers should do? But there's some girl in the village who might help out, though I don't think I shall leave them as much with her as I did Sharon. Sharon was very good with them. She'll make a good mother herself one of these days.'

Kara glanced at her in faint alarm, but it was a perfectly innocent remark.

'And now I suggest you go and get ready. You seem to have made quite a hit with the Tranakas family. And I'm glad for you. I was so afraid you wouldn't enjoy your holiday, this is such a quiet peaceful island.'

Peaceful? What a joke that was! She had not had a moment's peace since she arrived.

Kara decided to wear her pink silk again. With its silver and pearl embroidery it was nice and dressy and would give her the confidence she needed. For Aleko's parents' sake they would both need to hide their hostility.

As on the last occasion a car was sent to fetch her and she arrived at the Tranakas villa at eight precisely. This time, though, Aleko was not on the steps to meet her. A poker-faced manservant led her indoors and she followed him through the house and out on to the well-kept lawn at the back. There was quite a gathering.

Sophia and Nikolaos, Aleko, Petros and—to Kara's amazement—Katina. Her heart missed a beat. What was going on here? And Katina's father, with a tall handsome woman who was presumably his wife.

Aleko was the one to stand and welcome her. He strode across and taking her hand raised it gallantly to his lips. His dark eyes observed her closely, but there was a hint of amusement on his lips. 'Welcome, Kara. You are alone, I see?'

'Which is just as well,' she hissed. 'It's quite some party, isn't it?'

He grinned unconcernedly. 'It would have been more fun if your sister had come.'

'You swine!' she spat savagely.

'It's a pleasure,' he mocked, and pulling her arm

through his he led her towards the others.

Their greetings were warm and sincere. 'Is Sharon still not well?' asked Sophia. 'I was very sorry to hear about her illness.'

'She's a lot better, but not strong,' replied Kara. 'Actually she's talking about going home.'

Petros's head jerked and although she did not look at him Kara knew his eyes were upon her. She hoped he felt as rotten about it as he deserved. He was a typical uncaring male, thinking only of himself, wanting a good time but heedless of the consequences. It was to be hoped Katina knew exactly what she was letting herself in for.

Nikolaos handed her a glass of chilled wine and Kara sat in the empty chair next to Katina. Not that she wanted to sit by the girl, but Aleko had taken the only other empty seat.

Katina, on the other hand, seemed pleased to see her again. 'Hello, Kara. I thought you'd gone back to England?'

'Not yet,' answered Kara pleasantly. 'Aleko was short-staffed and asked me to do some work for him—so I'm still here.'

'Do I say, lucky you? Or is it terrible?' Katina wrinkled her tiny nose. 'I've heard Aleko's a tyrant to work for.'

Kara shrugged. 'He's not exactly easy-going, but it's different from what I'm used to, and actually I'm quite enjoying it.'

'Don't let him hear you say that, or he might try to keep you on permanently,' chuckled Katina. 'You haven't met my mother, have you? Mother, this is Kara whom I told you about. Kara, my mother, Phrosini.'

Phrosini Tranakas bore no resemblance to her tiny daughter. She was tall and statuesque, a fine-looking woman with her dark hair drawn tightly back from a face that was a fraction too plump. She held out her hand. 'I'm sorry I missed you the other day. If you have time you must come and see us again.'

Kara murmured something non-committal, said a few words to Thimios, then sat and quietly sipped her wine.

She noticed the way Katina kept looking at Petros and thanked her lucky stars that Sharon had not accompanied her tonight. What a fiasco it would have been!

And then out of the blue Katina said, 'I must admit it was a shock when Petros told me he loved your sister.'

Kara's eyes widened. Katina did not even sound as though she was upset.

'I realise now that it was not love I felt for Petros, not the sort of love between two people who want to get married,' continued the pretty dark girl. 'I love him as a brother and he loves me as a sister. It's all very simple. I hope he and Sharon will be very happy. He is so disappointed she has not come tonight. Me too. I would have liked to meet this girl who has stolen my Petros's heart.'

CHAPTER TEN

KARA continued to stare at Katina. It was incredible. It was unbelievable. It was the best news she could possibly hope to hear. 'But I thought—you and Petros were—planning to get married,' she stammered.

'They were dreams, silly dreams, something I had taken for granted,' smiled Katina. 'I love Petros, yes, but in a different way. He does not set my heart on fire. I do not go to pieces every time he looks at me. He is my very best friend, but that is all. I know that now.'

Kara caught Aleko's eyes on her. Did he know what they were discussing? Did he know about Petros and Katina? His expression was enigmatic, but it was as though he was reading her thoughts. And Kara unwittingly felt that magical thrill Katina had said was missing from her relationship with Petros. Why was life so cruel? Why did she feel attracted to a man who had made her life a misery from the word go?

She dragged her eyes with difficulty away from his and looked again at Katina. 'I don't know whether to say I'm happy or sorry for you.'

'Please,' said Katina strongly, 'feel happy about it. I am going to Rome next month to start a new job. I suppose I shall see even less of Petros and Aleko. But I shall be living with my aunt and will hear all the news.'

At that moment Sophia stood up and announced that it was time to go inside for dinner. They filed in two by two, Thimios leaning heavily on his wife's arm, Aleko escorting Kara.

'What were you and Katina talking about so

163

intently?' he asked, draping his arm casually about her shoulders.

She glanced at him sharply, and tried to ignore her fluttering pulses. 'As if you didn't know!'

'Petros?' he enquired.

Kara nodded, wondering if he knew what his touch was doing to her.

'She's told you they are no longer lovers?'

'I don't believe they ever were,' she said coolly.

'And now you're hoping that Petros and your sister will get married?'

'Naturally.'

'I do not want my brother to be coerced into a marriage he is not ready for.'

Blue eyes met brown. 'I don't think Petros would marry my sister against his will,' she replied firmly. 'He phoned her yesterday. That's hardly the sort of thing he would do if he wasn't interested.'

Aleko's eyes narrowed. 'He told Sharon about Katina?'

Kara shook her head, her lips compressed. 'Sharon wouldn't speak to him.'

He smiled and she could almost imagine him saying, 'Good for her!' She was glad they had reached the elegant dining-room.

Her relief was short-lived, however, when she found herself sitting between Aleko and Petros. She would have liked to speak to Petros alone, and she knew he wanted to talk to her, but it was impossible without Aleko overhearing.

Nevertheless it was an enjoyable evening. Sophia and Nikolaos were superb hosts and Kara was never allowed to feel that she was a stranger in their midst.

Her opportunity to speak with Petros did not come until they had retired to the lounge for coffee. There were two chairs a little apart from all the rest and as if with a single thought they made for them. The rest of the family were so busy discussing some new wine that was being developed that she and Petros did not even need to lower their voices.

'Katina has told me—about you and her,' she said. 'You've no idea how relieved I am. I really thought, this morning, that you were trying to tell me you were marrying Katina.'

He looked hurt, clearly wondering how she could have made such a mistake. 'It is your sister I love. Katina and I have discovered that what we feel for each other is no more than friendship. And I am sure my parents would not wish us to marry under those circumstances. I hoped Sharon would come tonight. I wanted to tell my parents about us.' He lifted his chin proudly. 'We shall have a beautiful baby.'

'They won't mind?' asked Kara anxiously.

'They will be disappointed about Katina, naturally. It was expected of us. And it will be a shock about the baby. But so long as I assure them I love Sharon and she me, I do not think they will be upset.'

'I hope not, for both your sakes,' said Kara quietly.

'Aleko is suspicious of everyone,' continued Petros. 'I cannot blame him for feeling as he does. But I have told him how much I love your sister, and I do not think he will oppose us any longer.'

Kara wondered when he had told his half-brother. Possibly only tonight, otherwise Aleko would never have invited them both to the dinner party. She smiled to herself. Petros must have quite spoiled his fun!

'Will you tell Sharon that I will be calling on her tomorrow night?' asked Petros. 'I wish I did not have to wait so long, but I must go to work. I do not want to anger Aleko.'

'Yes, I'll tell her,' answered Kara. 'You're very lucky—another few days and she would have returned to England.'

Petros's hurt showed. 'I have done that to her? I did not mean it. But I had to sort myself out. I was not being fair on Katina.'

'Your views or Aleko's?' she asked drily.

He shrugged. 'Does it matter?'

Kara supposed not, but it seemed to her that Aleko interfered in Petros's life far more than was necessary.

She glanced across the room and again Aleko's eyes were upon her. She clenched her teeth and looked away, wishing she had never met him.

As they sipped their coffee Katina wandered over to them, and then Aleko strolled across. The two younger ones moved away and Kara was left alone with him again.

'So it's all sorted out,' he said. 'All you have to do is tell your sister Petros is a free man and we shall soon be hearing wedding bells. Lord, I hope Petros knows what he's doing.'

'And what's that supposed to mean?' snapped Kara. 'Surely you don't still think that my sister's lying?'

Her voice rose and she saw Sophia glance across at her. With an effort she smiled and tried to pretend they were having a perfectly ordinary conversation.

'It may interest you to know that Sharon's breaking her heart over Petros,' she grated through her teeth. 'She was so distraught about Katina that she asked me to book her flight back to England.'

Aleko looked suitably impressed. 'Maybe I was wrong.'

'You know damn well you were wrong!' she cried. 'We're not all gold-diggers. You've obviously been associating with the wrong type.' But what would he care, so long as he was having a good time?

'I think we ought to go outside to continue this conversation,' he said, 'unless you don't mind everyone listening?'

She looked up and saw that they were the centre of attention. Blushing furiously, she shot to her feet. 'I'm sorry,' she said to the room in general, 'I think it's time I went. Thank you, Sophia and Nikolaos, for inviting me, it was a lovely meal.'

Then she turned to Thimios and his wife. 'It was good to meet you, Phrosini, and you again, Thimios. Goodbye, Katina. Good luck with your new job.' She smiled at Petros. 'I'll pass on your message.'

Without even glancing again at Aleko she swept out of the room, but he was on her heels and instead of allowing her to leave the house he caught her arm and urged her along the hallway which led to his own rooms.

'No, Aleko. No! Let go of me, will you! We have nothing further to say.'

'Have I told you before how beautiful you are when you're angry?' He smiled imperturbably. 'Your eyes sparkle like sapphires and you look more desirable than ever.'

'No matter how I look you're not taking me in there!' shouted Kara as they reached the door. She knew how easy it would be to give in.

'I thought we were discussing your sister?' His face was a picture of innocence.

'We'd finished,' she snapped.

He inserted his key into the lock. 'I've had a hectic few days, Kara, I need to unwind, and how better than in the company of a beautiful woman?'

'Go to hell,' she crisped. 'I'm not available.'

He smiled pleasantly and pushed open the door. 'I won't force you to do anything you don't want to do.

Haven't I told you that many times before?' He sat her down in his cool comfortable room. 'Can I offer you brandy, wine, more coffee?'

'If I must I'll have coffee.' Her eyes warred with his, but not until he had disappeared into the kitchen did some of the tension go out of her. She heaved a sigh and sat back, curling her feet beneath her, letting her eyelids fall. The next thing she knew the coffee pot was on the table and Aleko was sitting watching her.

Something stirred inside her stomach when she met the sensuality in his eyes, and for just a second she wanted him with an intensity that frightened her. Then she swung her feet down and sat up. 'I'm sorry, that was very rude of me.' She stifled a yawn.

'It was remiss of me to work you so hard that you fall asleep all over the place,' he corrected. 'Are you very tired? Would you like me to take you home?'

Kara knew deep down that she ought to say yes, that she might later regret staying, but a glow had developed inside her and she did not want to move. It amazed her how easy it was to forget the despicable things he did.

'I'll stay a while,' she said quietly.

He looked pleased, his eyes warm, resting first on her flushed face and her over-bright eyes, then moving slowly down her body, lingering for a few moments on the thrust of her breasts through the pink silk.

Kara felt them harden almost as though he were touching her, and her stomach muscles tightened as he continued his slow appraisal. Her dress had ridden halfway up her thighs and it was too late now to tug it down. She suffered his eyes on her, knowing what it was that he was saying, feeling an ache in her loins as she helplessly responded.

'How about that coffee?' she asked huskily, needing to break the threads that were being spun from him to her. If she didn't he would ensnare her as easily and as securely as a spider traps a fly.

'I'm sorry.' His voice was a low deep growl and even as he leaned forward to pick up the pot he did not take his eyes off her.

Kara felt her heart begin an urgent rhythmic beat and she wanted to move, but it was as though he had hypnotised her and she couldn't.

Then he looked down to pour the coffee, and Kara shifted in her seat and tugged at her skirt until it covered her knees.

'Why did you do that?'

His eyes met hers again and she lifted her shoulders. 'It was getting creased.'

It was a feeble excuse and he knew it. A smile pulled at his lips. 'You're trying very hard not to let me get through to you?'

Resignedly Kara nodded.

'Why?' He paused in the act of pouring the coffee, watching her, waiting for her reply.

'Because whenever we're alone like this all you think about is sex,' she protested feebly.

Aleko nodded slowly. 'Can I help what you do to me?' After a second's pause he continued, 'And you, what do you feel? Does your body respond as mine does to yours? Weren't you as anxious as me to get rid of all those people? I'm not suggesting we make love, Kara, though heaven knows how much I need it. I just want to be with you, to look at you.'

Which was as stimulating as actual physical contact. He could make her bones melt by a glance, every nerve and pulse scream. He stirred her most intimate places without lifting a finger.

'You know it does,' she whispered. It was so easy to

respond to Aleko. He had a mystical power that defied resistance.

'That is good,' he said, completing his task and handing the cup to her. She felt sure it was no accident when their fingers touched, and when her hand trembled so much that the coffee spilled into the saucer he sat back in his seat smiling.

Kara took a sip of the scalding liquid, and held on to her cup and saucer for dear life. But it was like clutching at straws. They were no defence against Aleko.

What game was he playing? Was this a slow seduction so that when the moment came she would be ready?

'What are you thinking, *agape mou*?'

She looked him straight in the eye. 'I'm wondering what it is that you're after.'

'Does there have to be something?'

Kara nodded. 'I can't believe you're prepared to condemn me one day and then accept me another. So whatever you're feeling has to be superficial.'

'You think I'm just after your body?'

She nodded. 'You wouldn't first of all try to cut my holiday short, and then miraculously extend it, if you didn't have some ulterior motive.' She deliberately made her tone curt.

'I wonder whether your opinion of the male sex will ever change?' pondered Aleko. 'How deep do your memories go? How long is it since your husband died?'

'Two years,' she admitted.

His brows rose. 'So long? I did not know. It's certainly long enough for you to have got over him. Not all men are the same, I can assure you. I would never, ever, be unfaithful to the woman I married. I think I told you that once before?'

Scorn lifted her brows. 'I'm not talking about marriage. I'm talking about carnal desire—lust—

lechery—call it what you like. That's all that's in your mind, and don't try to deny it.' Her voice grew louder. 'You've lusted after my body ever since we met. You disgust me, do you know that, it's all you're ever after! I was right in the very beginning when I said you were the same type as my husband.'

Aleko's eyes darkened ominously, a muscle jerked in his jaw, and his big hands clenched as though he would like to hit her. 'I am sorry you think that about me. Drink your coffee and I'll take you home.'

Kara immediately regretted her outburst. 'I didn't mean that.' There was pain now in her voice. 'I apologise. I know you would never bring our relationship down to that sort of level.' Making love with Aleko was a beautiful experience. Every touch, every word, every sensation, was pure ecstasy.

He looked at her long and hard. 'I can forgive but not forget. Your opinion of me must be very low. Perhaps I deserve it, I don't know.' He emptied his cup and set it down on the table, then he pushed himself up and walked over to the window.

Kara wanted to follow and slide her arms around him, but what good would that do? He would either take her in anger, or reject her altogether. She wanted neither. She wanted him to be tender and caring, she wanted to be rendered helpless, she wanted him to love her, as she loved him.

It was the first time she had admitted to herself that she had at last fallen over the brink and was in love. It was a painful realisation because it was a love that was doomed. Especially after what she had just said.

He swung round, his eyes as hard as bullets. 'So what do you want to do?'

His harsh tone did not give her much choice. 'I think I ought to go after all,' she said quietly, rising to her feet and picking up her bag.

'As you wish.' He followed her to the door, and she was so conscious of him behind her that her love for him was tearing her heart out.

'Aleko——' She swung round and faced him.

'Yes?' His face was an implacable mask, and her heart plummeted. Nothing she could say would alter things. She had hurt his pride too deeply.

'Nothing.' She clamped her lips and made her way out of the room. The best thing she could do was fly home to England as soon as possible, cast Aleko out of her life and out of her mind.

Neither spoke until they were in his car. Kara's whole body throbbed, and she wondered whether it really would be that easy to forget him. He had made such an impact on her. He had loved her and hurt her. He had been kind and he had been cruel. But despite all this, he had somehow captured her heart.

'How much longer will it be,' he said, totally disrupting her thoughts, 'before Rosemary can come back to work? I imagine Sharon will now make a miraculous recovery?'

His derogatory tone made Kara wince. 'My sister is already feeling much better,' she announced primly. 'But if it matters that much to you I'll insist that Rosemary returns tomorrow. She won't take much persuading. So far as she's concerned the sun shines out of your eyes.'

He looked at her with a frown.

'I don't mean that she doesn't love her husband,' added Kara quickly. 'She simply sees you as some godlike figure, some superhuman being. Lord, she doesn't know the half!'

Her disclosure seemed to amuse him, for his lips curled at the corners. A typical male, fumed Kara.

Flatter his ego and everything else was forgotten, but hurt him, and there was hell to pay!

The journey back to the Hythes' seemed endless, but at last they arrived. It was completely dark, only a silver moon radiating over the landscape. He turned to her. 'I'm sorry it's had to end like this.'

Kara stiffened and something inside her snapped. 'Are you?' she retorted furiously. 'Have you forgotten that you called me and my sister little gold-diggers? Because if you have, I haven't. You insulted me far more deeply than I have you.

'For the first time since Greg died I was really beginning to feel that perhaps life was worth living, that maybe I was being unjust in thinking that all men were the same.' She snorted indelicately. 'But not any longer. I'm not sorry after all for what I said. I meant every word, and I'm glad—glad, do you hear, that I shan't be seeing you again. Goodbye, Mr Tranakas!'

She scrambled out of the car and raced into the house, desperate to retreat to her room and break her heart. When her sister barred her way at the top of the stairs she scowled and tried to push her to one side.

'Kara, please, don't rush away,' said Sharon reproachfully. 'I have something to tell you.'

With an impatient sigh Kara slowed and stopped, turning to eye her sister. 'I'm sorry, I'm a bit upset at the moment. What is it? At least you're looking better, I suppose that's something to be thankful for.'

'You'll never guess,' smiled Sharon happily. 'I'm not pregnant after all. It was a false alarm!'

CHAPTER ELEVEN

KARA beamed her delight, all thoughts of Aleko gone. Hearing her sister was not pregnant was marvellous news. 'That's wonderful! Oh, Sharon, you must be so relieved?'

Sharon nodded. 'At least I won't have a permanent reminder of Petros. I never thought, Kara, that he'd back out like this. You were right when you said men weren't to be trusted.' Her blue eyes flashed fire. 'I hate them!' she finished vehemently. 'I'm never going to go out with one again!'

This was a wildly extravagant statement, Kara knew, and she smiled. 'Wait till you hear what I've got to say, you'll——'

'I don't want to hear anything,' cried Sharon. 'Petros can marry Katina with a clear conscience—I'm well rid of him!'

'Sharon, will you listen!' Kara took her sister by the shoulders and gently shook her. 'Petros isn't going to marry Katina.'

Sharon's eyes widened, but she looked suspicious.

'They've had some long talks and decided that what they feel for each other is nothing more than brotherly and sisterly love. Katina's got a new job in Rome, and Petros wants to marry you.'

The younger girl's eyes grew wider still. 'He's told you that?'

Kara nodded.

'Whoopee!' Sharon hugged her sister and did a little

jig on the spot. Then just as suddenly she grew sober again. 'He's probably only doing it for the baby's sake. When he discovers there isn't one, he won't want to know.'

'I don't think so,' said Kara reassuringly, even though the thought had crossed her mind. 'He's at last realised how much he loves you.'

'And I love him!' sighed Sharon, pressing her hands eloquently to her chest.

'He's coming to see you tomorrow night. He was very hurt when you refused to speak to him on the phone.'

'Serves him right,' cried Sharon, though she smiled. 'He shouldn't have gone away without telling me. God, I was hurt! I've wept buckets.'

'I know,' said Kara softly. 'I know what it's like to have the man you love let you down.'

'I guess Greg hurt you even more,' admitted Sharon ruefully. 'I've been pretty selfish these last few days. I'm sorry.'

'It's all right,' urged Kara, hugging her sister. 'I'm over him now. '

'Do you—fancy—Aleko?' asked Sharon intuitively.

Kara grimaced and nodded. 'But it's pointless. He wants an affair, that's all.'

'Oh, Kara, what a pity!' Sharon clung to her. 'It's the first time I've seen you enjoy a man's company since Greg died. I am sorry.'

Kara closed her eyes. She didn't want to talk about it. 'It's just one of those things. If you don't mind, I'd like to go to bed. It's been quite an evening, one way and another.'

Her thoughts as she lay and watched the silver moon-shadows across her bed were mixed. It was a relief, there was no doubt, to hear that Sharon was not going to have

Petros's baby, but it really did not matter any more. He loved her and wanted to marry her, and probably he would be disappointed.

But it was Aleko who was uppermost in her thoughts. What would he say if he knew she was in love with him? Lord, he wouldn't be able to get rid of her quickly enough. That wasn't in his plan of things at all. Perhaps it was for the best that she had caused this rift. The sooner she booked her flight home the better.

The next morning Rosemary tapped on her door early. 'Sorry to disturb you, Kara. I just thought I'd let you know I'll be going to the office today. Sharon's almost her normal self.'

Kara smiled and nodded, pushing her hair back from her face. 'I know. I saw her last night.'

'I wonder what was wrong?' Rosemary frowned, then shook her head, as if it didn't really matter. 'Have a good lie-in, Kara. I feel so guilty about disturbing your holiday.'

But Kara jumped out of bed the moment Rosemary had gone, showering and dressing, and then phoning Corfu airport. Unfortunately there wasn't a flight until the following evening.

With two full days stretching ahead Kara decided to spend as much time as possible with Sharon. Her sister was tremendously excited and chattered constantly about Petros, and the twins were so happy she was better that they made even more demands on her than usual.

But even so the time dragged, and when Sharon went out with Petros that evening, and the Hythes left for a dinner party with one of the men Geoff worked with, the minutes positively crawled.

She read a book and did some packing, but all the time her thoughts were still with Aleko. What would have happened, she asked herself for the thousandth time, if she had not ruined last night?

But always she came up with the same answer. He would take what he wanted and then say goodbye when the time came without so much as a twinge of regret. She was better off without him.

Her last day dawned. Sharon came bubbling into her room before she had even got out of bed. 'Oh, Kara, I'm so happy! It's all sorted out. We're going to tell Petros's parents tonight.'

'They'll be delighted, I'm sure,' smiled Kara. 'If Petros had gone to them in the first place none of this would have happened. It's Aleko who caused all the trouble.'

She wondered whether he still thought she had been after his money. Not that it mattered. Within a few hours she would be off the island and once back in England she could take up the threads of her old life.

It would be a repeat of when Greg died, except that this time she would be starting afresh with an even firmer resolve. Men brought her nothing but bad luck. Or was it that she always attracted the wrong type?

The day went even more slowly than yesterday. The Hythes were disappointed she was leaving and made her promise to get in touch with them when they returned to England.

'Take care,' said Sharon, when Kara finally snapped the last lock on her case. 'Give my love to Mum and Dad. Tell them I'll be writing.'

'They'll be thrilled, I know,' said Kara.

A taxi took her to the harbour and Geoff had arranged for a fisherman to ferry her across to Corfu. It was a shock, therefore, to see Aleko standing on the jetty instead, the engines running on his magnificent cruiser.

Kara eyed him aggressively, doing her best to suppress the sudden frenzied beating of her heart. 'What are you doing here?' She had hoped to get away without seeing him again.

'At your service, ma'am,' he smiled, tipping an imaginary peaked cap. He wore white drill trousers and a navy and white shirt and looked every inch the part.

'You're going to take me to Corfu?' she enquired disbelievingly.

Aleko inclined his head. 'I thought it would be more comfortable than sitting in the bottom of a fishing smack.'

'I prefer that to your company,' scorned Kara. What a lie that was! Her whole body craved for him.

His thick brows rose. 'You've made it clear many times what you think of me, you don't have to repeat yourself. Nevertheless I'm still too much of a gentleman to let you go in a smelly little boat. '

'That's rich!' exclaimed Kara, realising that attack was her best form of defence. She had conditioned herself to not seeing him again and now he had caused an expectant ache that would be difficult to assuage. 'You're no gentleman. You're——'

'I know.' His lip curled derisively. 'I'm a swine, and a bastard, and anything else you'd like to call me, but that doesn't alter the fact that I'm taking you to the airport.' He picked up her cases and strode on board, and she had no alternative but to follow.

She stood at the rail, her back stiff, wondering why he was going to all this trouble.

'Your sister has swung it, then? Her little ploy worked.' His tone was suddenly harsh over her shoulder.

Kara turned and frowned, not realising instantly what he meant. And then it dawned on her. So this was the

reason he had decided to give her a lift. One last chance
to gloat.

'I might have know what interpretion you'd put on
it,' she said bitterly. 'You've got a mind like a sewer!'

'Are you suggesting that she did not deliberately time
her announcement until after Petros asked her to marry
him?' he asked coldly.

'Of course she didn't. What the hell is it with you
Tranakas men that you think everyone's after your
money? Sharon genuinely thought she was pregnant.'

His lips curled. 'It's surprising how many girls chase
rich men.'

Kara's brows rose smoothly upwards. 'So you keep
saying. But I wouldn't chase you if you were the last man
on earth.' She swung back to the rail. 'In fact I don't
want to speak to you again. I've had enough of you to last
me a lifetime!'

He was instantly silent. Not another word was spoken
all the way. Kara wanted to look at him but did not dare.
She had no way of knowing whether he was angry or
amused, whether he felt like shaking her or kissing her.

When they did arrive she discovered that he was grim
and hostile, which pleased her no end. She made no offer
to help, letting him tie up the boat and carry her bags,
hail a taxi and check in her luggage.

He stayed with her until her flight was called and then
very correctly shook her hand. It was impossible to read
the expression in his eyes. He could have been a
stranger.

'Goodbye, Aleko,' she managed huskily.

'*Cherete*, Kara.' He looked at her long and hard, then
turned on his heels and disappeared.

Kara felt tears prick the back of her eyelids, but
determinedly dashed them away. This was no time for

sentiment. It was over, all over, and the sooner she
accepted it the better.

The flight was delayed at the last minute, the journey
tedious, and London wet. When she finally got home
Kara was tired and miserable and wanted only to go to
bed.

Life took on the same pattern as before. She had
learned to hide her feelings and no one, not even her
parents, guessed that anything was wrong.

When she told them about Sharon and Petros they
were at first worried and then happy, phoning their
daughter and offering her their congratulations, asking
when they were going to meet their future son-in-law.

'There's a wine festival in Birmingham in two
months' time,' announced her mother, satisfied. 'He's
coming over then to represent their company, and
Sharon's coming with him.'

Which meant that Aleko had changed his mind about
attending, even though he had such high hopes of
introducing their wines. Was it because of her? Kara
dismissed the idea instantly. Aleko was a business man
through and through. What had happened between
them would make no difference. He must have decided it
was time to give Petros more responsibility.

Long day followed long day, and Aleko was never out
of her thoughts for many minutes at a time. She
wondered whether she would ever forget him.

Sharon wrote frequently, sounding so happy that it
made Kara feel worse. They hoped to get married at the
end of the year, planned to honeymoon in Paris and then
live in private quarters at the Tranakas villa until their
own house was built.

Kara knew her friendship with Aleko would never
have developed into anything like that, but if only she

could have come home with happy memories, instead of this empty feeling of despair.

Gradually, though, she grew at peace with herself. There was no point in hungering after something she could never have. And soon it was time for Sharon to come home. Petros was going straight to the festival and then joining her here for a few days, before they both returned to Lakades.

Her sister looked bronzed and beautiful and very, very happy. 'Petros's parents send their love,' she said to Kara. But there was no message from Aleko, and in front of their parents Kara could not ask.

But when they finally went to bed she posed the question that had been trembling on her lips. 'How is Aleko?'

Sharon shrugged. 'The same as usual, so far as I know. I never see him.'

Which was no help at all. 'Has he finally given his approval to your marriage?'

'If you mean, has he accepted that I didn't deliberately set out to trap Petros, yes, he has.'

Kara's eyes widened. 'That's good news at least. How did you manage it?'

'I've no idea,' replied Sharon. 'I know he and Petros had some long talks, but Petros never actually told me what was said. I must admit they do seem to be getting on better, and I couldn't believe it when Petros said Aleko was sending him to England.'

'Nor could I,' admitted Kara. 'I remember doing a letter for Aleko saying he would be attending. I wonder why he changed his mind? You don't think it was because of me?'

'I shouldn't think so,' said Sharon offhandedly. 'There's no chance that you'd meet.'

'I suppose not,' said Kara sadly.

Sharon gave her a knowing look. 'You're still in love with him, aren't you?'

Kara nodded. 'Unfortunately. But enough about him. Tell me more about your wedding plans. Mum and Dad were relieved you want to get married here—I think they thought you might have a Greek wedding.'

Sharon smiled and Kara could not get over how radiant she looked. 'No way. We're going to make all the arrangements while Petros is here. His whole family will come over, including Katina.'

They both laughed and began talking about bridesmaids and wedding dresses, and Aleko was not mentioned again. In fact during the two weeks of the festival Sharon seemed to deliberately avoid bringing him into the conversation. Kara guessed she was doing it for her sake, but it made her realise how hungry she was for news of him.

The day after the festival ended Petros was at home when Kara got back from work. He was in the sitting room with her parents and they were plying him with questions. He looked happy and at ease, and the moment she walked into the room he stood up and gathered her into his arms. 'Kara, it is so good to see you again!'

'You too, Petros,' she laughed. 'I'm happy for you both.'

He nodded. 'We are happy too—very happy. And your parents, I think they like me. It is a great weight off my mind.'

Mr and Mrs Lincroft joined in the laughter.

'Where's Sharon?' asked Kara, finding it strange that her sister was not glued to Petros's side.

Petros and her parents exchanged glances. 'I think,' said the young Greek, 'that she is in the garden. Perhaps

you should go and find her? I have brought some wine—
one of ours, naturally,' he grinned, 'and we must drink a
toast. We have been waiting only for you.'

Kara hastened outside—then came to a sudden heart-
stopping halt. Aleko! No sign of her sister. Just this man.
What was he doing here? Had he been to the wine
festival after all? Why hadn't Sharon said?

He was facing her, as though he had been waiting. She
slowly advanced, her eyes never leaving his face, her
heart thudding now inside her breast. God, he looked
magnificent! He wore a pale blue suit and a white shirt, a
darker blue tie and shoes, but they hid none of his
muscular power or his virility, and her whole body cried
out for him.

Not until she was within a few inches of him did Kara
stop. He had not moved a muscle. Only his eyes searched
her.

She could not help herself. She had thought never to
see him again. 'Oh, Aleko,' she cried, 'Aleko!' And flung
herself at him, her arms around his waist, her head
buried in his chest.

His touch on her shoulders was light and he let her
give vent to her emotions without any similar response.
And gradually the enormity of what she was doing came
to her. She was making a complete fool of herself.

'I'm sorry, Aleko,' she said, drawing back, looking
down at her feet and wishing herself a million miles
away.

He lifted her chin with a forefinger. 'What was that all
about?' There was the suspicion of a smile on his lips.

Didn't he know? Couldn't he see that she missed him
like hell? That she loved him with every fibre of her
being? Kara groaned inwardly wondering what on earth
to say.

'It looks as though you are pleased to see me.'

She nodded dumbly. What was the point in denying it? She had already given herself away.

'Which is a very different story from the day you went away. I remember then that you said you never wanted to speak to me again. You'd also accused me of lusting after your body. What's brought about this sudden change?'

'Damn you, Aleko!' she hissed. 'You must know how I feel about you.'

'I know you find me physically attractive,' he admitted. 'Is that what this is? Are you in need of a man?' There was mockery in his tone now. 'I hardly think this is the right place. But if it will——'

Kara aimed her palm at his face, but he caught her wrist easily, and twisting it behind her back he brought her hard against him. 'Tell me, Kara,' he said, his tone low now and urgent, 'tell me exactly what is going through that mind of yours?'

Her eyes could not escape his. They were locked and held and she could read nothing of the thoughts in his head. But he was not entirely immune, that much she did know. His body throbbed against hers and she felt a frantic quickening of her pulses. She hoped her parents weren't watching.

She could fight him no longer. What the hell did it matter? She had admitted it to herself, why not to him? He would be gone soon, and she was so used to rebuilding her life that surely she could start all over again? Of what significance was it?

'I know you're going to think me a fool, Aleko,' she said, 'and if you weren't insisting, I would never admit it. But the truth is——' she nervously licked her lips, 'I love you. There now, I've said it, and you can have the last laugh. It's hilarious, isn't it, me loving you? After the way you've treated me. You've called me everything under the sun and yet still it's here.' She banged her heart with a clenched fist.

'It's painful, Aleko, I admit that. And I wish you hadn't come. I'm trying to get over you. It's hard, and it will take a long time, but I'll do it in the end. I will, I know I will.'

Tears were streaming down her cheeks now and she could hardly see his face. But her wrist was freed and his arms slid about her, and she felt the pounding of his heart and the heat of his body, then their mouths met and her head felt as though it was going to burst.

They kissed like hungry animals, all their needs and desires of the last two months culminating in this one glorious moment of fulfilment. Kara did not stop to think why Aleko was reacting in this manner. She thought of nothing except the joyous magic of being held in his arms once again.

'Kara, my own sweet Kara!' Finally he put her from him and gazed wonderingly into her eyes. 'I've been wrong, so very, very wrong. I've been cruel, and unmerciful, and I deserve every single harsh word you've ever slung at me. I love you too, Kara, with all my heart. And I find it no easier to admit this than you did.'

He drew her towards the garden bench and they sat down, well out of view now from the house, and he kissed her again. Kara could not believe her happiness. It was a miracle. She touched Aleko's hair and his face and his lips, and he caught her fingers between his own and pressed them to his mouth.

'I don't know what to say, Kara.' There was a humility about him that she found endearing. 'Ever since Cleo I've been afraid to let myself love anyone else.

I didn't want to get hurt again. I liked you from the start, but I couldn't see any future in it.'

'So you chose to cast me in the role of gold-digger?' There was hurt still in Kara's eyes. 'Did you really believe it?'

'I suppose I made myself,' he admitted sadly. 'Though I know now that you're nothing at all like that. You're a sweet kind girl whom I've made very unhappy. Can you ever forgive me?'

'You made Sharon unhappy too,' she accused quietly.

He grimaced and nodded, looking thoroughly ashamed of himself. 'I've already made my apologies. As I've told you many times, Petros and I have had our fair share of fortune-hunters, and Sharon isn't the first girl to insist that she's pregnant. It's an old trick. And I truly thought that Petros would marry Katina one day. Now I can see how wrong I was. Petros has grown up all of a sudden and I'm very happy for them.'

'She's forgiven you?'

He nodded. 'She's so much in love she would forgive me anything—at this moment. I hope my day of reckoning will not come later.'

Kara laughed. 'I doubt it. Did Sharon know you were in England? Have you been to the wine festival?'

He laughed and nodded. 'I made her swear not to tell you.'

Kara understood now why her sister had been reluctant to discuss him. Another thought struck her. 'Sharon didn't tell you, did she, the way I felt?'

'About me?'

She nodded.

'She knew you were in love with me?' he frowned.

'I told her, yes.'

'She never said a word. How I wish she had! I wanted to tell you how I felt the day you left. That was why I insisted on ferrying you to Corfu. But somehow I couldn't bring myself to do it and ended up censuring your sister again instead. When I knew I'd blown my chances I decided to wait until the festival. With a bit of luck you would have forgotten all the harsh words I'd said and remember only the good times. And they were good, weren't they, Kara? I'll never forget the night you crept into my bed.'

'It was one of my best mistakes,' she grinned.

'God, was I jealous when I learned you'd spent your honeymoon on Corfu! My body was racked with pain every time I thought about it. I can't believe that you can love me after the way I've treated you.'

'I do, and I always will,' whispered Kara, melting into him, lifting her face for yet another hungry kiss.

'What do you think your parents would say if we made it a double wedding?' he suggested, when they finally surfaced for air.

'I think maybe we'd better ask them,' she smiled. 'Which reminds me, they're waiting to drink a toast.'

'My toast will be to us, my sweet. To Petros and Sharon, of course, but from now on you're the most important person in my life, and we'll drink a toast every single day to remind us of how nearly we lost each other. All through my own stupidity.'

Aleko stupid? Kara would never agree to that. He was gorgeous and sexy, and he would never let her down. She had at last found the man of her dreams.

Coming Next Month

1111 AN AWAKENING DESIRE Helen Bianchin
Emma, recently widowed, isn't looking for romance. But a visit to her late husband Marc's grandparents in Italy seems like a good first step in picking up the pieces of her life. She certainly isn't ready to deal with a man like Nick Castelli!

1112 STRAY LADY Vanessa Grant
Since her husband's death, George has felt that she doesn't belong anywhere anymore. Then Lyle rescues her from her smashed sailboat and makes her feel at home in the lighthouse. But to kindhearted Lyle is she just another stray?

1113 LEVELLING THE SCORE Penny Jordan
Jenna had once loved Simon Townsend—a mere teenage crush, but he has never let her forget it. So when she has a chance for revenge, she takes it. Simon, however, has his own methods of retaliation....

1114 THE WILDER SHORES OF LOVE Madeleine Ker
She'd never thought it would happen to her—but almost without knowing it Margot Prescott turns from a detached reporter of the drug scene to an addict. Adam Korda saves her. But the freer she becomes of the drug, the more attached she becomes to Adam.

1115 STORM CLOUD MARRIAGE Roberta Leigh
Sandra has always known Randall Pearson. He was her father's faceless deputy, and has only once surprised her. One night he asked her to marry him. She'd refused then, of course, but now four years later Sandra is doing the proposing!

1116 MIRACLE MAN Joanna Mansell
Lacey is happy with her safe, sexless relationship with her boss—Marcus Caradin of Caradin Tours. Then he asks her to go on a business trip with him. Suddenly, in the exotic surroundings of India and Nepal, it isn't safe anymore....

1117 ONE CHANCE AT LOVE Carole Mortimer
Dizzy's family background made her wary of commitment. Zach Bennett is the first man to make her want to throw caution to the winds. But her position is awkward. Because of a promise, she has to conceal her real nature from Zach.

1118 THERE IS NO TOMORROW Yvonne Whittal
Despite her plea of innocence, Revil Bradstone despises Alexa because he'd once caught her in a compromising situation. Now he threatens vengeance through her employer. Desperate, Alexa is ready to promise him anything!

Available in October wherever paperback books are sold, or through Harlequin Reader Service:

In the U.S.
901 Fuhrmann Blvd.
P.O. Box 1397
Buffalo, N.Y. 14240-1397

In Canada
P.O. Box 603
Fort Erie, Ontario
L2A 5X3

Temptation™

TEMPTATION WILL BE EVEN HARDER TO RESIST...

In September, Temptation is presenting a sophisticated new face to the world. A fresh look that truly brings Harlequin's most intimate romances into focus.

What's more, all-time favorite authors Barbara Delinsky, Rita Clay Estrada, Jayne Ann Krentz and Vicki Lewis Thompson will join forces to help us celebrate. The result? A very special quartet of Temptations...

- Four striking covers
- Four stellar authors
- Four sensual love stories
- Four variations on one spellbinding theme

All in one great month! Give in to Temptation in September.

Harlequin Superromance

**Here are the longer, more involving stories you
have been waiting for... Superromance.**

Modern, believable novels of love, full of the complex
joys and heartaches of real people.

Intriguing conflicts based on today's constantly
changing life-styles.

Four new titles every month.
Available wherever paperbacks are sold.

SUPER-1

HARLEQUIN SIGNATURE EDITION

VIOLET WINSPEAR

HOUSE OF STORMS

Editorial secretary Debra Hartway travels to the Salvador family's
rugged Cornish island home to work on Jack Salvador's latest book.
Disturbing questions hang in the troubled air over Lovelis Island.
What or who had caused the tragic death of Jack's young wife? Why
did Jack stay away from the home and, more especially, the baby
son he loved so well? And—why should Rodare, Jack's brother,
who had proved himself a man of the highest integrity, constantly
invade Debra's thoughts with such passionate, dark desires...?

Violet Winspear, who has written more than 65 romance novels
translated worldwide into 18 languages, is one of Harlequin's best-
loved and bestselling authors. HOUSE OF STORMS, her second title
in the Harlequin Signature Edition program, is a full-length novel
rich in romantic tradition and intriguingly spiced with an atmosphere of danger and mystery.

Watch for HOUSE OF STORMS—coming in October!

HOFS-1